D. THOMAS GOCHENOUR

Party in JEDDAH

ISBN: 978-1-966615-38-5 (Hardback)
ISBN: 978-1-966615-39-2 (Paperback)
ISBN: 978-1-966615-40-8 (E-book)

Contents

Early morning after the party

It was earliest dawn in the narrow dark canyons of residential buildings on Lutfiya Street, not one of the poshest districts of the city of Jeddah. The mu'ezzin had just moments before made the call to Dawn prayer and there was still no one on the streets. There was still another hour and a half to sunrise but already it was humid and very warm, without a puff or draft to cool the streets or the dim canyons between tall buildings.

At this time a little boy, maybe six, maybe seven years old, poorly dressed in a dirty tee shirt that once had been white and a white skirt which was also soiled and fell down to just above his ankles and wearing pink soled flip-flops, entered Lutfiya Street, still rubbing his eyes and idling moving about picking up litter here and there and hoping to get five or ten halala coins from any of the kindly doormen who might already be awake and might notice him. The boy was perhaps six or maybe seven years old but of slight build and short for his age. He needed this pocket money because at home he did not get enough to eat and he had found this was an easy way to earn a riyal or maybe more. He ambled pointlessly and slowly up the street, looking to shoo the cats, and on some occasions, but not on this day. a rat. He was in no hurry, he had three more long dusty streets to walk through and the baker's shop, where he could buy a flat loaf of fresh bread for 20 halalas, would not be open until just after sunrise.

On this morning he idly walked up to house number 11, a massive white concrete house that loomed close over the street and sat behind a low brick wall that was topped by the bars of wrought iron fence topped off with the sharpened points of iron finials which altogether wall and fence came up to a height slightly taller than the boy, maybe a meter and sixty centimeters high. It was not a fence that would seriously challenge an intruder or thief wanting to break into the building. The boy passed this way many times and he liked to think that the vertical metal bars with sharpened points were so many spears on display for his inspection and he would run his right hand over them as he passed by the house. He did this on this dark barely twilit morning on a Sunday in late April, hardly looking up or in front of him. The building's doorman did not come out of his cell and there were no lights on in the cars parked in the open ground floor under the building where the residents could park their cars in the shade during the day. So no one saw the little boy.

On this morning, he was more than half way down the fence when he was abruptly stopped by a white- skinned foot in his way at about his eye level. He almost ran into it. He looked up alarmed and surprised and then saw that the foot was connected to a white, gleaming woman's leg, and there was another one next to it. And the leg was connected to…. he was shocked to see the hairy crotch of a mature women, the shameful private area of a woman, which he had spied once or twice on his older sisters, and once on his mother and for which he had been beaten on the head for such a vile act. He stared in shock and dismay at this hairy mound, which did not have the black curly hair like his sisters' had but had light colored hair. He stood stoke still. He dared not so much as even touch the foot hanging in the air by his eyes. And then he looked further. This was a whole, naked woman lying arched over the spear points and not moving. How could a white woman be so brazen and shameless as to be naked to the whole world to see he thought. His eyes settled on the breasts, and their light-colored areoles. They were not big, not like his mother's. And above them limply hung a gray bra which had straps still hanging over the woman's shoulders. He could not see much beyond them because the head was bent back behind this woman's shoulders. And then he ran his gaze back over the body down to the woman's vulva so close to his eyes—he didn't know that this part was called a vulva, he didn't know at all what these private parts were called except that they were secret and shameful parts that only women had. He also found them unattractive and repellant to his eyes.

Altogether it must have been only a few moments that he had stared, dumbstruck, at this sudden apparition in the night. He had never seen a naked white woman before in his life. Her skin was so translucent and almost glowing, so unlike his sisters', and it seemed as white as the fat on a sheep's tail. He began to feel some movement in his private part, an unfamiliar sensation of arousal, and then he began to feel something much more visceral and alarming. It was fear. What he was doing was forbidden and wrong. He was scared something bad would happen to him because he was looking at this woman. And then he noticed that flies were swarming around this woman's body around her stomach, some even were bumping against his face and trying to fly into his still gaping mouth. He swatted at them and shut his mouth. And that is when he noticed that two of the spearpoint finials had somehow pierced through the woman's torso from the back, looking just like the spear points jutting through the fish that were caught with spearguns down on the strand. And as the dawn had become just a faint bit lighter, he noticed drops and driblets of blood. And his eyes followed one of the paths of blood down the side of the woman, and on the brick wall and down to a small puddle of blood right near his right foot. At this time he also noticed for the first time a pair of white panties lying in the dust on the pavement next to his left foot.

Now the boy was terrified. This was something hugely sinful and wrong. He did not know how to call what he had seen. But something very bad had happened here and he should definitely not be looking at it. His father would beat him very seriously if he ever knew. He stopped looking at the woman's vulva and turned his head away from this awful apparition. He looked up the walls of house number 11 to see if there were any lights on. There were none. He was now breathing fast and swatting away the flies from his face, looking all around to make sure no one saw him, that no was looking at him. He turned and began to run back up the street the way he had come. He hitched up his skirt in one hand so he could run faster and he lost his flip flops after only a few tens of meters running. He ran all the way up the narrow street to the main street which was heavily lit with orange street lamps and there he turned and continued running the thirty or forty meters further to a second intersecting street where he turned right and ran on fifteen meters further to the station of the district shurta, the civil police.

He wasn't sure what he was going to do or say. He would probably get beaten once he told them. He ran up the stoop and hardly noticed a shurta officer standing and leaning against the wall next to the door, smoking a cigarette. The officer leaned over and with his arm tried to arrest the boy's flight toward the door. Amusedly he barked at him, "Whoa, where do you think you're going?" He thought he could make sport out of this street waif, but then he noticed the boy's wan face and eyes opened very wide in obvious terror and fear. He stooped down. "Tell me, what's happened? What's scared you? Did you see a rabid dog?"

The boy was breathing too hard to say anything. He pointed vaguely back the way he had run.

"No, don't worry. No one's going to hurt you. No one will beat you here. Let's go in and tell the serjeant what you saw. Okay?"

They entered the police station. Around the shift serjeant stood three other shurta officers in their dark khaki uniforms with shoulder epaulets leaning toward the boy and waiting for him to tell them what it was he had seen or what had happened to him. He stuttered out that he had seen a white woman and that it was shameful. And that there was blood. And that she did not have any clothes on. And it was shameful and sinful to look upon her.

"You saw a ghost? Of course, of course. Settle down. Is this what you just saw? Was the woman dead?"

The boy nodded. And then he shook his head. He didn't know if she was dead. He had no idea what a dead, naked white woman looked like.

"Where did this happen?"

The little boy did not know the street name. He again waved his right arm vaguely in the direction he thought was right. "Three lanes over."

"Can you take us to where this happened?"

The boy's eyes grew wide again with fear and he shook his head violently. "No, I won't go back there. Not ever again. It's too awful. Hateful sight."

"Do you think what you saw was on Hamid Lane? On Abu Umar al-Khamidi Lane? On Lutfiya Street?" The boy nodded. "It's building number 11." He spluttered out.

"Okay, we'll go there without you. Can you stay here and wait for us to come back?"

"No." The boy was afraid that the shurta officer would tell his father, and then he'd have to face all hell of a beating.

"In that case," the serjeant said as he leaned over in his chair, "Muhsin, give him some chocolate and a bottle of water. And we'll all be on our way. Hamdi, you and Sa'ad go to Lutfiya, number 11 and report back to me at once." He leaned back toward the boy and handed him two shiny brass 25 halala coins. "Go buy yourself some bread at the bakery." The serjeant knew why little boys were out on the streets before sunrise.

The boy left the station after the shurta officers and he wandered further down the well-lit street until he stopped and sat down on the curbstone. He took another drink of the chilled water and then he began to cry. The skies were beginning to turn pale grey with dawn's advancing twilight. It was now sweltering hot.

The Investigation Opens

Bonny was only half asleep on the large blue couch in the middle of the vast area between the living room and the dining area when there was a sharp rap at the main entry door. She heard it as if coming from far away, like a bell in a distant tower, but she knew it was the door. She had been sleeping fitfully and having frightful dreams for some time. She was sweaty and felt hot even though she had neither blanket nor sheet over her. And she had felt a cracking headache for some time and felt sores everywhere which added to the ghastly aspects of her dreams. The apartment was very warm even though the air conditioning was going full tilt. In the summer the AC could only cool the apartment to 30 degrees Celsius and now it was probably warmer than that.

She stood up and her head began to throb even worse. She had a hangover like she rarely ever had had before. It was that sweet home-brew red wine that Ken made. Easy to go down especially when chilled and filled with fruit for a sangria, but poisonous the next day. She slipped her feet into her fabric sandals almost losing her balance and then picked up her blue satin house robe. She was wearing only a sheer short nightgown. Her mouth was sticky and her eyes too, the eyes wanted to remain closed. She rubbed at them as she shuffled over to the door. The apartment was dimly lit, sunlight was on the edge of the balcony, she could see. And the four big floor fans were whirring away in the living room, but didn't seem to chase off the stuffiness.

Who could be at the door at this obvious early hour? The doorman from downstairs? He didn't do that often. Most likely a guest who had stepped out and locked himself out or had forgotten something and had come back. She feared the visitor would knock again before she got to the door. She rubbed her eyes again as she reached for the doorknob expecting to see Husny, the doorman, on some trivial excuse for a visit.

But she was surprised when she opened the door inwards to see a light-skinned Arab man dressed smartly in an unconventional style: a light brown khaki colored uniform with epaulets with a red honor bar on the collar of his short-sleeved shirt. The epaulets had on them several golden stars or golden crowns or something like that indicating high rank and there was a collection of colorful service bars above his chest pocket. He wore a black beret with a golden round badge on it, instead of the more usual red-checked keffiya. He sported a pencil thin neat black moustache but had a clean-shaven chin. He was lean and slender, not tall, barely taller than Bonny. She only ever expected to see Arab men in their white dishdasha robes and keffiyas.

"Good morning, madame. I suppose I woke you. I'm Chief Investigator and Deputy Prosecutor of Section C, Colonel Adil al-Kuthaimi an-Najrani. You can call me Colonel Adil." He stepped into the apartment and took a couple of steps toward her. Bonny stepped back three steps somewhat surprised by his aggressiveness.

"Are you the owner of this apartment? Is the man of the house here?" Adil said in a flat, nasal American accented English which had always irritated Bonny whenever she heard Arabs speaking it.

"Yes. Eh no. My husband Ken rents the apartment. I don't know the name of the owner, but he is Saudi." said Bonny. Colonel Adil had a pleasant expression on his face but he was looking around the apartment as she said this. He then focused on Bonny.

"And what is your name?"

"I'm Bonny Addison. In my passport it is Elizabeth Stewart Addison. I suppose you want to see it?" Then Bonny noticed that Adil was staring at her breasts and her pudendum and she realized she had no underwear on under her sheer nightgown. She closed her satin robe and wrapped one arm over her bust and the other over her pudendum. How annoying she thought. What cheek to stare at her private parts like that.

"Is your husband here? Can you get him down here?"

"Well, I don't quite rightly know where he is. Presumably Ken, Ken Addison, is in the bedroom upstairs." But she didn't say that presumably he was in bed with that Danish girl.

Colonel Adil again was scanning the apartment almost as if looking through Bonny.

"And you had a big party here last night? Is that right?"

Then Bonny realized that there were empty bottles of wine and whiskey standing on almost every surface around the apartment as well as the mostly empty punch bowl on the dining table right near them. She had not cleared anything away before collapsing a few hours earlier, and neither had their maid, Sunithra.

"What time is it, might I ask?" said Bonny trying unsuccessfully to show irritation.

Colonel Adil made an ingratiating smile and said chirpily, "It's probably about seven o'clock in the morning by now," with the tone of a man who was long accustomed to getting up in a bright mood and going about his business long before that hour.

Bonny moaned slightly. Her headache again was throbbing painfully.

"Hang-over?" Colonel Adil said in a friendly way as he signaled with his left arm to people who were collected beyond the open door. Into the apartment came ten or twelve people, maybe more, in dark brown khaki uniforms who looked more like the shurta police she was accustomed to seeing so often everywhere around the city, on the streets and by mosques and government buildings. These shurta police were more like the usual Arabs of the Kingdom, dark skinned and complexioned, and with beards or scraggly stubble on their chins and jaws. Except for two women who were in the group. She always saw these motley police and thought of the Keystone Kops. How ridiculous they looked: one like Muslim zealot with a thick black beard, another very tall and slender like a volleyball player, and several positively fat looking like some many Sancho Panchos. She did not like that they were now all tramping into her house.

Without even thinking about the additional self-incrimination she said, "Yes."

"You're English, aren't you? And your husband is too?" It was easy to recognize the English accent. The English expats who worked in Jeddah always sounded so snooty and condescending toward him when they spoke to him or anyone else Arab. He wondered if they were even ruder when they spoke to his darker skinned officers when encountered on the street.

"Yes."

Colonel Adil spoke something in Arabic to someone in the group, waving his hand over toward the sliding glass doors of the balcony. His Arabic voice was gentle and sounded like birds chirping together in low voices far away. Two officers with black cases went over to the open sliding doors and stepped into the light on the balcony and began searching there.

"So. I see you had a party here last night?" he addressed her again in English.

"Yes there was. What is it you want? What are you doing here? Because of our party? There were surely no complaints." Bonny recovered her equilibrium a little and tried to become aggressive with Adil and wanted to push all these Arabs out of the apartment. She knew that the rest of apartment building was empty, the flat immediately below them unrented, and the second floor flat belonged to a foreign couple who were on leave and out of the country.

Colonel Adil smiled, just momentarily. "It seems we discovered early this morning that a crime had been committed here overnight. Just outside your apartment building. Most likely one of your guests was killed. We found her body outside where it shouldn't have been, and she was a white skinned European. We'd like to know her name and find out how see got into that awful condition. Not at all the usual case of crimes we have in this neighborhood. Ever. So we need to search this apartment to see if we can find the perpetrator of this abominable crime."

Bonny gasped. And then winced as her headache again began to throb hotly.

"You perhaps should take some aspirin." said Colonel Adil. "How many people were at the party?"

Now Bonny was looking around the apartment to gauge the extent of the damage that was on display.

"I don't know exactly. Fewer than twenty. Maybe twenty-five at the most. I didn't know everyone who was here." Bonny could see that two of her Danish nurses were sleeping together on another large sofa in the living room. They were wearing only their underwear and were embracing one another. And she could see someone's arm draped over another sofa which faced away from them. It was the dark-skinned arm of a man.

"And how many people are there here now?"

"I don't know. I guess I passed out around four in the morning."

"Here looks a bit like a sort of debauchery." Said Colonel Adil. "Or maybe you had an orgy? Everyone got smashing drunk? Right? And then you all set out to screw and copulate one with the other and swapping partners through the night. Had a great time?" Colonel Adil's smile was now synthetic and sarcastic.

Bonny looked across the twenty-five meters at the two officers out on the balcony. One was photographing the sofa that was out there standing against the low wall. Another appeared to be dusting on the railing, as if taking fingerprints. It was bright outside.

"Better for you if you don't answer those questions. But it does appear that your wild party ended in murder. We'll search the apartment now. Better you sit back there on that couch and be still and keep quiet. It may take a while."

"Can I go to the toilet?" asked Bonny.

"Yes, but Sabiha will join you to assure that you don't try to escape or something." He spoke to a young dark-skinned woman, whose face seemed hidden by her uniform and wore her black beret as if it were a shower cap.

"Oh, for God's sake. I need to pee." Said Bonny now completely annoyed with this soft-spoken boy, because she realized he did not look even thirty years old. He was certainly no Omar Sharif, although he seemed to be trying to be suave and dashing.

"Feel free, but come right back here. Sabiha will go with you. Whether you like it or not. We can't have you trying to escape acccountability here." He said a few more words to the woman who had stepped forward. She was surprisingly plump and short, and her trousers were cut too long.

"Now, we'll begin to search the house for other party makers still here." Said Adil in English, as Bonny shuffled to the toilet with Sabiha behind her.

He turned to the others and addressed them in rapid Arabic. He gave detailed instructions. "We need to film people as we find them now. We will not knock on doors, do not wake the occupants before you've taken photos of their situations. Afterwards you can wake, take their names, and once they are standing—don't let them get dressed until you've taken their photos standing today. Full on, just as they are. They can use their hands to hide their private parts if they are completely undressed. After that let them get dressed and we will lead those who are upstairs to come downstairs here. We'll take samples down here and record their identity cards then. Let's start first with the people who are on the couches here in this big room. Remember try not wake anyone, at first. Now let's break up into three teams. Salim, you can photograph now the bottles of wine and liquor, wherever you see them. Don't move any of them. And also photograph the bottles that are there in the trash cannister."

It seemed every one of the shurta police had in his or her hands a camera as well as a hand gun on his or her belt. Adil took another look around at the scene and shook his head. What a scene of abomination and debauchery, he thought. Truly disgusting. Westerners are really abased, like savage animals without shame or morals. They were all obsessed with fornication, he thought as he had observed many times before, even in his days in America. He walked over to the next closest couch where two tall, slender white women were asleep deep in the embrace of each other. They both were wearing only panties and skimpy bras. Their mouths were wide open, and one of them was lightly snoring.

He pointed to one of the men closest to him. "Take these photos. Get different angles. Now let's get the others. These we'll call women two and three." On the next large sofa whose back was to the interior of the apartment it was apparent that a man and a woman were together sleeping under a sheet. It wasn't clear if they were dressed or not. The man looked to be an Arab or a Middle Easterner, while the woman, although dark haired appeared to be a European. They took several photos here.

"So, make a note. This is man number one, and woman number four." Adil said in Arabic. He went on to the next sofa but it was unoccupied.

And then a fourth sofa and again there was a couple, a man and a woman on the sofa in close embrace. The sheet had mostly fallen off of them and they appeared to be completely naked, and unmistakably European. And on the final couch, there was a sleeping Arab man—a young man, but clearly a married man from the gold wedding band on his ring finger, sleeping in the arms of a white woman who had no clothes on. "This is going to go badly for all these people," muttered Adil to himself in Arabic. "The Arabs should know better," he thought. "This one looks Palestinian." On the last sofa he looked at there was a sleeping woman dressed in street clothes with bare arms.

This was a disgusting scene, he thought again. Just what the Koran warned against and forbade. People who could carry on like this, in front of others, even in the privacy of their homes, could be sinners in many ways; they would not be the least bit upset if a murder occurred in their midst. They most likely didn't even notice or try to stop it.

Bonny came back from the toilet with Sabiha and went to sit down on the blue couch where she had slept.

"Wait a minute, Mrs. Bonny," said Adil. "Stand up and we'll take your picture. Just as we found you. You're woman number one. Did you have any non-alcoholic drink here at this party?" He spoke again to Sabiha in Arabic. She answered him with a clear affirmation and opened a small box that she had put down by the door when she had come in.

"There's water over there in that plastic bottle. Plain water." said Bonny.

"Okay," said Adil and then he addressed Sabiha again in Arabic. She went over to the table, picked out a plastic cup and took up the bottle and then she came over to Bonny and offered her two tablets of ibuprofen and poured her a cup of water. "Awfwan," said Bonny to Sabiha. Adil noticed: she had clearly meant to say 'shukran' (for thank you) and instead had said 'you're welcome.' And had mispronounced it too.

"Don't want you to suffer just yet." said Adil sarcastically. "We can save your suffering for later." He thought to himself, 'and you will suffer from the looks of things.'

"Now where are the bedrooms?" he said in English but not addressed to anyone in particular.

"There's one in the back. You can see its door there. And the haremlik bedrooms are upstairs along a corridor."

"And do you have a live-in maid?" Adil asked Bonny.

"Oh yes, of course. I forgot." answered Bonny. "We have a Sri Lanka maid. Her bedroom is on this level behind the kitchen. You go to the kitchen to get to it."

Adil thought to himself, 'Of course you forgot about the maid. She's dark-skinned, black like a nigger. You English don't count those as people.' He spoke to Bonny in answer, "Well we'll go in there last. She's the likeliest to raise a real screaming stink. We'll let her sleep for now. And which is the master bedroom upstairs?"

"The door the farthest to the left when you get upstairs."

"Fine, and before we start with that," said Adil, "we will begin to take some probes. First, the check for your blood alcohol level." He snapped at Sabiha in Arabic, who quickly brought over one of the boxes and took out a breathalyzer. It was a digital, black plastic breathalyzer with a white mouthpiece.

"Well, I'm drunk, and hung-over. You can see that yourself plainly." said Bonny, getting more and more irritated with Colonel Adel.

"We're just taking measurements."

"Can I get dressed now?"

"No. You'll have to wait a little longer. But may I suggest that you don't get any further UN-dressed? Where are your clothes, by the way? You clearly undressed to go to sleep. Upstairs in the master bedroom maybe?" He looked at the display on the breathalyzer which Sabiha was showing him. "Oh my, 0.25, you must've had eight drinks, or more even. You were really drunk. Was everyone drinking so heavily?"

Bonny didn't answer this question. She was stuck on the issue of how she got in her skimpy nightgown. "I don't know where I got undressed. I don't actually remember undressing for sleep."

"Fine. So if you'll excuse me." He instructed one of the teams to check on the downstairs bedroom, repeating the instructions he had given before to insure the proper procedure. And then he quietly went upstairs with the other two teams.

As he got to the first bedroom, he noticed that there was no keyhole on the knob, so it was likely that the room was unlocked. He quietly turned the knob and pushed the door in. He was thinking that he really hoped to catch the occupants in flagrante delicto, an expression he had learned in the U.S. at his advanced police methods studies. He liked the sound of the expression, but also he knew that it wasn't just for voyeuristic reasons. He knew that by Islamic law, to charge a couple with adultery and make the charges stick the couple had to be caught in flagrante delicto—in the blaze of the offense. But in this room he was to be disappointed.

In the large double bed there was a man who appeared to be naked turned on his side toward a naked woman's supine body. His bare back was to the door, and the woman appeared to be sleeping. A sheet covered them from their waists down to their feet. He was making curious movements when Adil's team entered and it appeared that he was licking the sweat on the woman's body around the sternum between her breasts which were rather flat. Adil signaled the photographer to start.

The man sat up with a start. "What's the meaning of this?" he shouted at them.

"Quiet now. Sorry to interrupt, but I believe you're committing adultery." said Adil in his flat unemotional English. "I'm chief investigator and deputy prosecutor of Section C for the city of Jeddah. I have to inform you in addition to committing a very serious crime in the Kingdom, that you also seem to be responsible for a murder which occurred last night during your party in this apartment. I presume you are Ken Addison, the tenant of this apartment?"

The man sat up and the sheet fell to his crotch baring his limp penis. The man appeared quite alarmed. The blond woman did not stir from her deep sleep.

"What do you mean a murder? What, here? When did this happen?" and then Ken began to move as if to get out of bed.

"Wait a minute." said Adil. And in Arabic he asked if his man had taken all the photos her needed. That man nodded his head. "Wake your woman up. We know she's not your wife. You probably know the law here about adultery. We need to take photos of both of you standing next to the bed just the way you are now. And yes, I said murder. An attractive white woman who looks or I should say looked like the woman who is now under you."

"She's Danish. And maybe the dead girl is also Danish. We had a crew of Danish nurses here last night. I'm Ken Addison, you're right. Dr. Ken Addison. I work at the King Fahd Community Hospital as chief surgeon, as does this lovely girl here. I mean she also works there. As a nurse." And Ken began shaking the sleeping Danish woman who began making the same incoherent noises that people often make when pushed out of a deep sleep. She was very slow to wake.

"As soon as my man here finishes taking photos of you two standing up, you may both get dressed. But I ask you to stay here until I call for you. You might think back over the period of your drunken orgy last night, about who might have killed that other unidentified—but possibly Danish—girl who was probably thrown onto the fence below your balcony in a state of complete undress. Sometime during the late night. I ask you not to try to escape, or slit your wrists in the bathroom, please." Then Adil went to the second bedroom. 'These are such disgusting, immoral people.' he thought as he led the second team to the door.

This time when he pushed open the door, he got just what he was hoping to find. "In flagrante delicto!" he whispered to himself. The camera man turned his camera to video mode and began at once filming. There, again on a very big—bigger than king sized—bed without any sheets to cover them there was a man on top of a woman, humping obliviously away, his back to them. The woman was making noises of rapture and undiluted pleasure that came in rhythmic barks in coordination with the regular, rapid humping of the man on top of her. Adil's camera man walked around to get a side view, first to the left and then to the right. Neither of these coupling creatures took notice as their eyes were shut tight, and they were both making utterances of pleasure.

Adil was almost at once concerned as he recognized that without question while the white woman in supine raptures was very possibly also Danish, the man making all the thrusting and heaving was no doubt an Arab, and most likely a Saudi Arab. This was the reason for Adil's concern, because this represented a very serious criminal procedure for him, a challenge which now he could not just ignore as a petty misdemeanor. This was a capital offense, and he had three other officers with him to act as the four witnesses he needed to send this unknown Arab man to his doom. He appreciated the danger that came with witnessing in flagrante delicto—in blazing offense. But he also realized that this act of copulation would get in the way of his conducting a murder investigation. He was going to have to interrupt this shameful act, he'd have to get them to reveal their identifies, and he would have to arrest both of them. This could be delicate. Adil was certain that the Arab man—knowing full well the consequences of adulterous fornication in front of the police—would make a fuss, if not actually put up a fight and offer serious resistance, and he would possibly have to be subdued, perhaps violently. He had no idea how the woman about to reach her climax would react. He hoped that she'd be quiet. He decided he'd have to leave all three of this team behind in the room to break this up and get the couple to cooperate. But first in a mild, sharp command, he told the man in Arabic, "Stop at once this sin against God and nature. Stop I say." And then a little louder, "Once again I command you to desist this shameful, sinful behavior. You are under arrest. As is the woman you are fornicating with!"

The man busy in copulation was slow to respond. But he opened his eyes and turned his head to one side. The woman didn't seem to respond at all, but her eyes were half open and her barking sounds of passion stopped as the heaving slowed to a stop on top of her. The man withdrew from her and pulled back covering his genitals with his hands. He didn't say anything. He lifted his legs off to one side and turned and sat up on the side of the bed.

"What is your name, you reprobate." Adil scolded in Arabic. The man did not reply, but looked up at Adil with a furious and sullen look on his face. "You know the consequences of your sinful act, don't you?"

The man nodded his head but continued to throw daggers at Adil through his eyes. To his other officers, Adil said, "You know the procedures. Get them to stand up next to the bed, photograph them and then get them dressed. And they need to find their ID cards too."

Then in English Adil raised his voice, "Hey you darling. My sweet Danish miss, you're guilty of fornication and adultery. Sit up and face your fate. What is your name? You're a nurse, aren't you?"

"Yes. Yes, I'm a nurse." the young woman said as she tried to pull herself up to a sitting position. She did not try to hide her genitals, nor to cover her breasts. "My name is Agnate."

"Very good. And what is this brute's name? Or do you not even know it?"

She finished getting into a sitting position next to the Arab man on the side of the bed. "He told me his name was Adnan. But I don't know his surname."

"Too bad for you. He's a VIP. Okay now, very good. I have to leave you two for a moment. But you can get dressed once we get some more photos. Please stand up there." In Arabic, he repeated the same in a sharp command aimed at the man. "You'll have to excuse me now. But first darling, tell me, were you all night with Adnan?"

"Yes." she said very softly her head nodded as if in shame almost doubled over down to her upper thighs. "Could you say that a little louder?" said Adil. "Yes." She said again.

Adil went to the first bedroom and asked two of his officers to accompany him to the third room with him, leaving one behind to observe Ken and his unnamed Danish girl who now were standing, still undressed next to the bed. This time at the third bedroom, when he pushed open the wooden door, the hinges squeaked throughout the entire swing of the door. He hated squeaky doors but in the humidity of Jeddah they were prevalent and in his own house he had to regularly apply treatments of WD-40 to the hinges in his house. The squeaking woke up the sole occupant of the bed. It was a young woman, also probably an Arab woman with smooth milk-and-coffee colored skin. She was wearing black lacy underwear and as soon as she realized it was a man coming in the door, followed by two other men, all in uniforms she screamed. And she continued to scream and her arms began to flail at them as if she were throwing invisible rocks at them. And in between hurling these invisible rocks she'd pull the sheet up to her neck to cover herself, screaming things in Arabic that even Adil did not quite understand.

"Take some photos," he said in Arabic to one of his officers. "No videos please."

After nearly a minute of screaming and wailing, Adil shouted in Arabic at the young woman. "Shut up. At once. Where are your clothes?" Stand up here, out of bed and be still. Young woman, you are in very serious trouble. So again, stop your wailing." Then in a lower tone of voice, he said. "If you are quiet and cooperative with our inquiries here, things will go better for you."

Eventually the young woman stopped flailing and screaming at them.

"Good, now step out of bed. Drop the sheet. We have to take one more photograph—shameful as it is. Good. Now that that is done you can get dressed. Are those your clothes? Where's your abaya?" The young woman grabbed up her clothes and held them against her body to cover herself and started as if to move to the bathroom door in the room.

"No, right here. So we can see you. Don't try to escape or jump out the window. We're on the sixth floor here."

Adil continued now in a gentler Arabic voice. Tell us your name."

"Khadija." the woman hissed at him.

"And your patronymic?"

The girl refused to say anything more as she buttoned up a dark blouse.

"Did you sleep with a man last night here?" he asked and then he signaled one of his officers to duck his head in the bathroom. He went over to the bathroom door and looked inside and then shook his head. There was no man in the bathroom. Khadija did not answer, but looked at

Adil with hatred and anger in her face. Adil thought it was a familiar looking face.

"If you won't tell me, we'll find out from your ID card." Almost at that same instant Adil saw an expensive, Italian purse on the floor next to the chair where Khadija's clothes had been. He snatched it up, opened it, and began ruffling its contents until he pulled out a cardholder.

"Here it is," he said to Khadija as he showed her the Saudi internal passport, her ID card. "It says, Khadija bint Abdallah Amr al-Mish'ari. Oh dear. The same Abdallah al-Mish'ari who is the deputy governor of Jeddah?" Adil knew this could be very problematic and difficult for him, the daughter of such an important and powerful man, head of the al-Mish'ari tribe, one of the most powerful in the Hijaz. He had to use the very most proper procedure and show sufficient respect. The young woman remained silent.

Then he looked again at the young woman who was still scowling at him in fury, and he checked the face against the photo on the ID. Then suddenly Adil knew why Khadija's face looked so familiar.

"Do you have a brother named Adnan?" Khadija's face took on an expression of surprise and dismay, but she did not answer. Adil knew however that her expression had answered for her where words were not forthcoming. He had detained two children of one of the richest and most powerful men in Jeddah who were both at this degenerate party where a murder had occurred, and he would have to arrest them on very serious charges. This could get very sticky for him. Politics were becoming more important than justice or the law.

Khadija had finished dressing and even put on a very expensive pair of dark blue, designer high heels. She was quiet and she was looking away from Adil. Maybe she was even beginning to sob. She was whimpering.

"Fine, come with us downstairs." said Adil showing her with his arm to the door. "Is your abaya downstairs?" he asked. She nodded and led the way out the room. Along the corridor, Adil stopped at each room and invited the other reprobates—now dressed in their party clothes—to also proceed downstairs. Dr. Ken tried to say something to Adil, but he waved off the Doctor. "Save it, for later." Adil said in English, not even looking at him. Adil followed the five detainees and his seven officers back down the stairs to the main room where now there were collected a crowd of people, some dressed, some with sheets wrapped around them. Bonny was still clutching her thin robe over her sheer nightgown.

"Oh I'm sorry Mrs. Bonny. You can get dressed now."

"I don't know exactly where my clothes are just now. What I wore last night. I'll have to go to my room to get other clothes. May I?"

"By all means." said Adil. "Sabiha if you'll again escort Mrs. Bonny." Bonny made for the downstairs guest bedroom and Adil at once said, "But isn't the master bedroom upstairs?"

"Yes, but my clothes are in that bedroom."

Adil took note. And when Bonny disappeared with Sabiha into the guest bedroom, he asked Ken. "Dr Ken, tell me. Do you usually sleep in the master bedroom where we not too long ago found you?"

"Yes, but I can explain."

Adil raised his hand and stopped him. "Have we roused everyone now?" Adil said as he looked around the room, counting to himself the nine people who were standing there to one side away from the five others from the upstairs bedrooms. His twelve officers stood spread out like a lasso around all the party goers.

In Arabic Adil asked in general, "Are we ready to ask for names? Have we started taking blood alcohol readings? No. Okay, Na'ima could you begin? Have we collected the house maid? No? Hamid you and Husayn go fetch her. In the servants' room behind the kitchen. You, you and you go and look in all the rooms we haven't seen yet and come back if and tell me if you find any men's clothes, purses, or other people we haven't discovered yet." Three men moved off and a woman, Na'ima, moved off in different directions. Adil wheeled around to his right, and in English addressed Dr. Addison.

"Dr. Ken, how many people came to your party last night? Can you name everybody here in the room now?"

"I'm not sure," said Ken. I think there were maybe twenty-five twenty-six people who came. But I'm not sure I can name them all. Some left early, some came as friends of people I'd invited."

"I'll have to ask you to make a list of all the people that came. If you please."

Then Adil turned to the two Danish young women whom he had previously seen embraced and sleeping on the big couch facing the dining area away from the balcony. "So now, I presume you two are Danish. As Mrs. Bonny said, part of the group of Danish nurses who came to last night's party. Did you have fun? Enjoy yourselves?"

The two Danish girls—one tall, blond and statuesque, and the other short and a little plump, sporting short cropped light brown hair, both dressed in colorful, light-weight summer clothes including shorts—both blushed a little, and one said that yes there were five of them that came last night. It was a very fun party.

"And what is your name, Miss Bluebell?" Adil continued.

"My name is Lisbeth Jorgensen."

"And mine is Vigga. Vigga Andersen." said the plump one.

"Like the writer of the fairy tales?" said Adil.

"Yes."

"Well, I like his fairy tales. They've been translated into Arabic and I read them to my little daughters all the time. Mrs. Bonny (who had just stepped out of the guest bedroom dressed in green long slacks and a darker green knit top) told me there were five of you. Now I have met you and Lisbeth, and upstairs, Else and Agnate, who are over there—all very attractive young women—but I don't see a fifth Danish nurse here. Who was the fifth member of your group?"

Lisbeth jumped in, "That would be Anna. She's not here."

"Yes, poor Anna." said Adil and then raising his voice and addressing seemingly no one in particular but at the same time everyone in the room. "Anna would be the poor girl lying now in the morgue of my forensic laboratory. She was killed, or murdered during this party, sometime before five in the morning."

Adil waited for the reaction from the seventeen party-goers gathered around the large room. "Now Dr. Ken here tells me that there were twenty-five to twenty-six people attending last night's festivities and drink-up. That means by my count that there are seven to eight people unaccounted for right here and now. I am presuming that it was a man that did in our poor dead Anna, but it appears he is not here just now. Do any of our Danish nurses remember who Anna was drinking with? Or dancing with last night?" He looked first at Lisbeth and Vigga who were standing close together, and then to his right at Else and Agnate who were not standing together, but who both stepped a little further away from their lovers of earlier in the night.

"In case you all did not understand, we are here just now not to ruin your fun and pleasure, but because one of your number, one of your colleagues was apparently murdered or killed before the party ended. And I imagine someone here must have seen the man who most likely threw her off the balcony, to her death. None of you noticed that? Were you all so drunk? Or were you all so heavily engaged in adulterous sex that no one noticed Anna?" He couldn't keep his feeling of frustration out of his voice.

"I saw her dancing with a man late." said Elsa. "They were dancing close and tight together. But I didn't recognize the man. He was wearing a yellow and black checked, short sleeve shirt. I didn't see his face."

"Oh, I saw that too." said a stout man in the back of the room nearest the sliding doors. "A couple dancing in tight embrace. He wearing a yellow and black shirt, and she was a tall blond, wearing white shorts."

Adil had seen this man earlier sleeping with a small obviously Arab woman, on the large gray sofa nearest the balcony. He was swarthy in skin color and he stood with his arm around the small Arab woman now fully dressed. Adil had assumed that this man was Arab and that he was another of the party's adulterers. He addressed the man in Arabic. "What is your name? And where do you work?"

"My name is Jameel Zagloul," the man answered in English. "I'm from Turkey. I'm an intern lab technician at the KFC."

"So you understand Arabic?" Adil said in English. "KFC now has lab technicians when they fry chicken?"

"No. I meant at the King Fahd Community Hospital. We call it the KFC. I understand and speak some Arabic because my wife here, Jameela, is Arab, from Jeddah. I said I saw such a couple closely embraced."

"Closely embraced, like you and Jameela were closely embraced when we first came in here?"

"Yes. Intimately embraced and dancing. But dressed in their clothes."

"Was this man big, tall, European, Arab, black-skinned, red-haired, bald, black-haired, familiar to you? Or what? Can't you describe him a little more that a yellow and black shirt?" said Adil in English.

"No. I can't"

"And you didn't see the two of the them going out on the balcony?"

"No."

"Agnate, did you see them go out together onto the balcony?"

"No. I went upstairs with Adnan not long after I saw them dancing, long before the music stopped."

One of the police agents who had been out searching on the balcony came in carrying a very brief pair of white shorts, legs cut up to the crotch, a pastel colored checked short sleeve shirt and a purse.

"Those shorts?" Adil addressed Jameel in English. "Hot short shorts?"

"Yes, like those." said Jameel.

"Sexy, wouldn't you agree, Jameel?"

"Yes, sexy. My wife would never wear anything like that, even under an abaya."

Screaming suddenly could be heard muffled through the kitchen. It was loud and sounded like some woman had been stuck by a sword, or had just lost a child in an act of violence.

In English Adil said to no one in particular. "I guess my men found Sunithra in flagrante delicto with some man. Mrs. Bonny, does Sunithra live in that room with her husband?"

"No. But there was a Sri Lankan man who came to help her with the party and the clean-up. But I don't think he's her husband. And I don't know if he is still there."

"Did Dr. Ken invite you to last night's party?" Adil asked Jameel.

"Yes."

"So you know Dr. Ken from work?" asked Adil stepping a little closer to where Jameel and Jameela were standing together, his arm still around her shoulders. "Yes." "But you didn't know the Danish nurses from KFC before you came to the party last night?" "No. I don't know any of the nurses at KFC, except my Jameela, here." Adil looked a little closer at Jameela who was maybe twenty centimeters shorter than Jameel. She looked also swarthy, like an Egyptian.

Adil addressed her in Arabic. "Jameela, please say, are you from Egypt?"

She answered him in Arabic. "No, I am Syrian."

"And are you married to Jameel?"

"Yes." She continued in Arabic. "We studied at university together in Turkey and married there. When I got a job here, he followed me here. And yes, we are Muslim."

Continuing in Arabic, Adil asked rather acerbically, "And as Muslims you are not uncomfortable making love together in front of these kafirs (unbelievers) and adulterers?"

"We were not copulating, and no we are not against sleeping together under covers, modestly, in front of these others who are mostly our colleagues."

"How much did you drink last night?" said Adil.

"We did not drink. Except for juice. Not wine, not whiskey."

"Well, we can see the veracity of this statement right now." Adil turned and instructed Na'ima to give the breathalyzer test to Jameel and Jameela. It showed negative blood alcohol for both of them.

"Record that," Adil told Na'ima in Arabic. Then he muttered out loud in Arabic, "A surprising result, I should think for this group of worshippers of Bacchus."

At that point, two of his agents came down the stairs. One reported in Arabic that there were no other people in any of the rooms or closets of the upstairs. The other said that he had discovered one bathtub in one of the bathrooms which was filled with fermenting red grape juice and distillation equipment. And lots of empty grape juice bottles. It was clearly not a bathroom used for bathing.

"Dr. Ken, to add to your crimes, you were making moonshine in your bathroom still?" Adil asked with some sardonic menace in his voice.

"No, we're making quality wine, not moonshine." It wasn't clear if Ken was trying to sound superior and condescending, but it came across that way. Ken was very angry with Adil and this intrusion.

In Arabic a very slight, lean ruddy-skinned man dressed in Western casual summer clothes, interrupted, "My wife and I didn't drink any wine either."

"Excuse me, what is your name?" Adil said as he turned to his right to look at a very short middle-aged couple, who could be Yemeni. The woman was dressed modestly in Western style with black slacks and a long sleeve white blouse. The man spoke with a pronounced Yemeni accent. And while there was a short very black beard on his chin and jaws, the hair on his head was salt and pepper. So maybe he was more than forty five years old.

"Ismail bin Ali al-Hibshi and my wife Fatima. We did not drink. We are Saudi citizens. We drank only juice also. And we went to bed, in privacy in the guest room there, earlier than most of these other guests."

"And Fatima, did you come to the party in an abaya?"

"Yes."

"And where is it now?"

"In the guest room, where we slept. All the women left their abayas there when they came. They're still there."

"So there you are, Khadija. Your abaya is probably there."

"Now Ismail bin Ali, did you notice this unknown man with a yellow and black checked shirt, who danced with a blond, scarcely dressed tall white woman during the party? Or did you Fatima?"

"No, by God, I swear I did not. Nor did I see such a man at all in the party, during the buffet or the games period."

"Well good. God bless you both. Fatima you can go get your abaya, and Ismail, when she comes back, you can both leave right now. I recommend to you not to attend such parties in the future, even if it is with colleagues you might think you know well."

The al-Hibshis left about five minutes later. Meanwhile the police officer who had been on the balcony had rummaged through the purse and found a wallet and extracted from it a residence permit card. "Here it is." He said as he handed it to Adil.

Adil looked at the card. And at the photo laminated on it. It looked like it could be the young woman he had removed from the finials of the fence a few hours earlier. "Anna Mergete Hensdattir." He read out loud in English. "Does that fit with the name of the fifth nurse?" He addressed Lisbeth and reached out and showed her the card. Lisbeth nodded her head.

"Yes, that's Anna. She came with us tonight. What an old-fashioned name. I always thought her family name was Hensen."

The other girls also confirmed that it was Anna. They all thought her last name was Hensen because she had always told them that was her name.

"Well, that is established. She is identified as the victim. Now we need to identify the man in the yellow and black checked shirt. Did no one see him step out onto the balcony after two o'clock with this Anna?"

There was silence. Then a young woman in the back of the group spoke up. She was a plump woman dressed in faded jeans and a thin cotton plaid short-sleeved shirt. She spoke with an American accent.

"I may have seen them, but I have no idea what time it was. I didn't answer before because I was unsure. You see, I had had too much to drink, I mean wine. And I apparently passed out."

"What is your name, please?" said Adil with his pleasant smile again on his face.

"Alison Plummer. I work at the U.S. consulate. I came with Walter Simms, as his guest. We sing together in the expat choral society. Someone must of (Adil noticed that she made that grammatical error that was so prevalent in the U.S.) put me on that sofa nearest the glass doors when I passed out. I came to briefly needing to go to the bathroom, and get some water too. When I went back to the sofa, this couple—I didn't see her, but she was followed by this big white man in that yellow checked shirt—they were just going out to the balcony through the open sliding glass door. I went back to sleep. I think he had curly, thick reddish hair."

In Arabic Adil addressed Na'ima. "Test her breath." Na'ima took the breathalyzer over to Alison and gave her the test. She then showed the apparatus to Adil. "I would say from this and your size that you probably had three or four glasses of wine." He said in English. "And then you passed out."

"That must be right." said Alison. "I'm sorry. I drank too much."

"Well good. Now we have to find out how we can contact Anna's relatives. Mrs. Bonny, do you have any ideas? You said the nurses worked for you." Adil was beginning to think that Bonny was like a procuress to these Danish nurses. He wondered if she brought her nurses to all of their parties to sexually entertain the men in the party.

"Yes. All of these girls were hired through the same placement agency, I mean the ones from Denmark, of course. I have the address in the hospital. We could contact them in Denmark and they should have Anna's parents' names and contact details."

"Are you the only one at the hospital who knows where to find this agency's contact numbers?"

"No, the human resources office has it. They hired the agency's services."

"Okay I'll send an officer over to get it. Had you trained these nurses with the law and customs of this land. Had you told them that adultery can be a capital offense? No? I thought not. Now let's test the Danish girls for blood alcohol levels. They seem to have been the life of the party."

Na'ima now went over to Elsa and gave her the breathalyzer. It read .22. "From my little table here and guessing your weight I would say you had ten drinks last night, Else. That's a lot."

"Scandinavians are noted for being heavy drinkers." she said not the least bit repentant.

"I would say so."

Agnate's measurement was somewhat less, only .15. "And you probably had six drinks?" said Adil. Agnate shrugged her shoulders but didn't say anything.

"Now try Adnan." Adnan first turned his head away from Na'ima and then put up his arm to block her.

Adil spoke sharply to Adnan in Arabic. "Look, you might get away with this in an ordinary traffic stop, but you will cooperate with our sample taking. You're going to jail as it is. We'll take blood from you by force using a needle if we have to. Now blow into the apparatus."

Adnan blew into the mouthpiece and Na'ima displayed the reading to Adil. It was .09. "That's not too bad for big boy like you." Adil said in English. "Maybe only four cups of wine." Still Adnan did not speak.

In Arabic Adil asked Adnan, "Did you bring young sister with you to this den of sinners?"

Adnan nodded his head. His eyes were still throwing daggers at Adil, who ignored them. Adil knew that soon he would be showing fear on his face.

"Excuse Colonel Adil," said Ken, "before we go any further, could I turn on the de-humidifiers and turn up the air-conditioning? It's getting very warm and stuffy in here. And maybe I could close the glass doors to the balcony, also? They let in the hot air."

"Oh, yes. Please do." said Adil. And in Arabic he told one of his crew to close the glass sliding doors. An officer bounded over to the doors and closed them. Ken walked over to a thermostat on the wall behind the dining table. Almost immediately there began a new noise in the room from the vents. Now in English Adil said, "Excuse me, as for comfort, you all can sit down now and we'll continue with our questioning in a more comfortable way."

The party goers started moving to the free couches and sat down all facing Adil who moved to the dining table where there were six bottles of French cabernet wine and four half empty bottles of single malt Scotch arranged around a large silver punch bowl which still had warm sangria in it and limp wedges of stained lemon and orange floating, the usual detritus of a drinking party the next day. Adil's foot bumped into something on the floor before he could sit down. He looked down.

"What are all these apples doing on the floor?" he asked in an alarmed voice.

Bonny answered. "They were important props for our party games. We use these games to break the ice early in the evening."

"Really? And how do you play this party game? You weren't playing strip poker or spin the bottle or those other idiotic games that fraternity students play in the States?"

"No, we take the apples out of the freezer where they get very cold and we had four teams, alternating men, women in a line." said Bonny with some relish. "Each team has to pass one apple to the next person without using his hands, and so on to the end of the line by holding the apple under the chin. And that is hard to do, because the apple is very cold on the neck, and everyone's laughing, and everyone's a different height."

"Oh, so a touchy, feely game where the men and women have to get close together. How did our married, conservative couples like this game? Jameel, did you participate with Jameela as a partner?"

"Yes. But the al-Hibshis didn't."

Hamid came back through the kitchen into the dining room leading a very short slight, very dark-skinned woman with oiled black hair and dressed in half of a sari wrap. There were trails of tears on her cheeks. Behind her was an equally small, dark man, probably also Sri Lanka.

"You are Sunithra, yes?" asked Adil. "Do you understand English?"

"Yes, sir, I am sir. Please, a little, sir. I speek only a leetel, sir. I do no wrong. No sin, sir."

"Well maybe. Are you married to this man here? Is he your husband?"

"Yes, sir. He is, sir. My betrothed husband. From Sri Lanka."

"Do you have a work permit? And do you have something that would prove that you're married to this man?"

"Yes sir. In my room. I can get them. But don't hurt him, sir."

"I won't, I assure you." Said Adil. He addressed Hamid in Arabic. "How did you find them?" Hamid answered that they were naked as Adam and Eve and in each other's embrace, sound asleep when they went in. "Did you take photos?" Hamid nodded. "Did the man show you his documents, his work permit or residence ID?"

Hamid held them up to Adil, who perused them carefully. Both work and residence permits showed that Sunithra and the Sri Lankan man were unmarried, and that each bore unique surnames, meaning that they were probably adulterers. Adil scowled.

"It looks to me, Miss Sunithra, that we have caught you in the act of adultery? Do you know what that is?"

Sunithra began shouting in a high shrill voice, and waving her arms. "Don't hurt Mathander. He's not to blame." Most of what she shouted was incomprehensible to Adil as Sunithra's accent was strong and her command of English grammar and vocabulary was obviously weak. What he did understand was near the end of her rant, when she said something like she was not a virgin because Dr. Ken had raped her in her room when she was showering, several times. But she had fought him. Still he had raped her.

Adil looked at Dr. Ken and then back at Sunithra. "I guess you have nothing to say about what Sunithra just said?"

"She's lying, of course. I never touched her. Not in her shower, not sexually, not anywhere in this house." Bonny was staring at Ken and her face seemed to indicate that she was shocked and inclined to believe Sunithra.

"Okay, you two sit over there," Adil directed Sunithra and he pointed to a free couch in the back of the living room.

In Arabic he spoke to Na'ima and Sabiha. "Carry on with the breathalyzer tests. Everybody. Record names. And make everyone produce their

IDs or passports or residence permits. People should be able to find them here."

Then he flipped open his iPhone and made an automated call. His deputy answered. "Has the medical pathologist completed his investigations of our blond victim?" Adil said in Arabic. "Fine, we will need here the presence of the two Rape forensic nurses. Can you call them and have them get over here as soon as possible, with twelve testing kits? And also you need to send over three prisoner vans, we're going to have a lot of arrests here. One will be for the women."

"Okay, can you transfer this call to the medical pathologist?"

"God bless you this morning, Abdallah. You've been checking our pretty, unfortunate Danish victim? We've found a name for her, from her effects here. She is Anna Margete Hansdattir, she was 28 years old, unmarried." He slowly spelled out Anna's name in English letters. Nearly everyone in the room was listening closely to Adil, even if they did not understand Arabic.

Then in English, Adil said something into the phone that only Dr. Ken understood. "Have the insects told us anything yet?"

"No? So that probably means that the time of her fall was not earlier than 3:30 if I understand you right. You agree?"

Adil switched back into Arabic. "Have you already tested her blood alcohol level? There was lots of drinking at this party last night."

"That's very high, don't you agree? She could have been unconscious when she fell or was thrown off the balcony, don't you agree?"

"Was she dead already when she fell off the balcony?"

"Then have you determined the cause of her death?" After a long pause, Adil said, "I see. Alright I will be there by noon, maybe you can report to me when I return. God give you peace." And he hung up his phone.

Adil took a handkerchief from his pocket and mopped his forehead. It was noticeably warm in the room, and Ken's adjustments to the cooling system hadn't brought down the temperature or reduced the humidity yet. Adil looked at his watch. It was nine-thirty. The two police women were still taking breathalyzer tests on the last of the partygoers.

"Now, I need to tell you what is going to happen today." Adil addressed the group. "We're going to do a complete search of the apartment. Including a search of your pockets, purses, or hand bags. We'll be looking for contraband or other illicit goods. "If any of you know of the presence of such illicit goods that you might have brought to this party, it might go better for you later if you tell us about them and where they are now."

"We will also need to conduct some tests on all of you, and I ask you to cooperate. Some of these tests will be delayed until the materials and the testing nurses arrive in about an hour."

"In the meantime, I will ask some of you further questions or interview you individually. And we'll need to write down in a list, your full names, date of birth, nationalities, address of residence, and place of work. All of this could take a few more hours, so feel free to ask for water. And I suppose that you could cut up and share eating the apples. Mrs. Bonny is there any more food left in the kitchen that people can eat if we get to afternoon?" Bonny nodded yes.

Then in Arabic Adil gave instructions to his men, sending three on searches of the ground floor and balcony and assigning four others to begin checking hand bags. He then turned to and addressed the man he had thought was a Palestinian whom they had found sleeping with a European woman. He spoke to him in Arabic.

"Your name is Subhi Muhammad? You look Palestinian, but your residence permit says you're Jordanian."

"Nearly all Jordanians are Palestinians."

"And you are aware that we found you this morning sleeping without clothes on with this woman, named Emily, who is not your wife? She was also naked. Did you fornicate with her during the night? Don't lie to me, because we are going to check if you're telling the truth."

"No, I did not."

Then in English he addressed a young woman with very white skin and obviously black-dyed long hair.

"And you are Emily Watford, from England. And you're not married to Subhi are you?"

"No."

"Did you come to the party with Subhi? I will tell you the same thing I told Subhi. Don't lie to me because we will find out in other ways if you have lied."

"No. I came with Walt. We know each other through the chorus."

"It seems that this chorus is a party center for expats in this city. Are there any others at last night's party who did belong to this chorus? You, and Walt, and Alison. And she said she knew Walt and she came with him as his guest."

"We all came in the same car. Bonny attends our chorus meetings, on Tuesday evenings."

"And you did not know Subhi before this party?"

"No actually we had met before at the choral club."

"Alright then. And considering the condition of undress we found you in in his embrace this morning, then you had sex together during the night?"

"No, we didn't. We slept on the same couch, you could see that."

"But my dear. Subhi told me that you two did have sex together."

Subhi understood the ruse Adil had played and with a start he jumped up from the couch as if to protest. But Emily broke down and she began to sob.

"Yes, then. Yes, we did have sex. Is that a crime, if you love someone?"

"To someone married if he is not your husband? I suppose it is. It is a crime in this country anyway. And in your country it's considered a sin, banned by the church. A very serious crime here. Even condemned in the Koran. Now if you two are married to each other, it is not so serious at all. But I'm afraid…"

Hamid came in from the balcony carrying plastic sandwich bags with something in them. "Excuse me," he said in Arabic to Adil, "We've found some joints of hashish on the balcony. They've all been smoked. And this one here has enough paper left that it looks like we might be able to recover lip marks or even DNA from it."

"Oh good. I wonder if more hashish might turn up." said Adil in English. "Sit down Subhi. I told you not to lie to me." Then turning back to Emily. "It doesn't matter if I played that little trick on you to get you to confess. We are going to perform a vaginal swab on you in a few moments. And that will confirm just who is telling the truth. But tell me, Emily. Did you see anyone smoking pot last night?"

"I hate you."

"I'm very crushed by that," said Adil in a mocking low voice. "And so, you did see some people smoking pot?"

"No. I saw some men going out to smoke on the balcony. I did not know whether they were smoking tobacco or pot. I assume it was pot."

"And who did you see smoking altogether?"

"It was Walt, and that man over there"—she pointed at Adnan—"and a short black man who I do not know and who is not here now, and another European man I do not know and do not see here now."

"And Subhi went with them?"

"Yes, and Subhi too."

"Yes, and Subhi too. But at that time, you did not see a tall foreigner with curly red hair and dressed in a yellow and black checked shirt out on the balcony? Perhaps smoking pot with these men?"

"No, I did not see him out on the balcony, then or later."

"And smoking the pot was early? At the time of the games? Or later at the dancing time when the music started?

"At the time when the dancing started."

"But Subhi didn't ask you to smoke with him?"

"No, we were dancing together when he excused himself. He knows I don't smoke at all."

"And finally, Emily. Answer me. You did not see a naked Danish nurse passed out on the couch out there on the balcony, maybe at about the same time when you and Subhi were beginning to snuggle together on that couch facing the balcony and closest to the doors?"

"No there was no such woman out by herself like that who I saw."

"Thank you. And Emily, how old are you?"

"I'm twenty-one. I'm visiting my parents while I'm here on semester break from Exeter University."

"Good." As he turned away from Emily, Adil thought 'English girl, only 21 years old, and already a racist and condescending snob in the way she talks to me. Probably comes from her parents' attitudes.'

Adil walked back to the far side of the living room and in Arabic addressed Adnan.

"So can you give me any hashish now? You're getting into ever deeper trouble, you know."

Adnan still refused to say anything to Adil. He shook his head in the negative.

"Who gave you the reefers of hashish?"

Adnan remained quiet. Adil asked one of his officers in Arabic if they had found Adnan's handbag yet?

The officer said that they had found it and in it was his Saudi internal passport, and two unsmoked joints of hashish.

"Was it your friend, the black man who smoked with you on the balcony?"

Adnan remained still and did not answer.

Adil leaned toward Khadija. "My dear, you told me you came here in the car driven by your brother. Was there a short black man in the car with you?"

"Yes, Saif. A friend of Adnan's from his office. He sat in the back seat."

"A driver did not drive Adnan's car here with the three of you?"

"No."

"And that would mean Adnan's car is still parked downstairs?"

"No doubt."

"Well, what kind of car does Adnan drive?"

A white Porsche Cayenne."

"Thank you. You don't know Saif 's family name?"

"No. I heard Saif Muhammad. But I don't know his family name."

"And do you think that Saif brought the hashish to the party?"

"I don't know."

Adil went to the center of the room. And in English he said to the group in general in a loud voice.

"Now everyone has had a breath test and given his or her name to my girls? Right? Now we can start the latest test we need. It's really quite simple. My girls will put an ordinary cotton swab in your mouth and rub it gently around on the inside of your cheek. And presto. The test is done. We won't take fingerprints here just now. Na'ima and Sabiha will start from the glass doors and move to this this end of the room."

"Are you taking DNA samples to test for each of us?" asked Ken in astonishment. He had come to develop a low regard for the Saudis, thinking of them as completely incompetent when it came to technical matters.

"Yes, we are exactly going to do that, Dr. Ken. Ever since some of our citizens started becoming martyrs as walking bombs, we have had to use DNA testing to discover who they are. It is useful in a lot of other crimes as well."

Then in Arabic he told Adnan to give him the key to his Porsche. Adnan scowled again some more but he took a key out of his jeans pocket and gave them to Adil. Adil turned to one of his officers and told him to go and open up the car and begin searching it, fingerprints, the works. He also told him to send the doorman up. The officer picked up one of the small boxes by the main entry door and left the apartment. At the same time a couple people stood up and came over to the dining table asking for water.

"Now Dr. Ken, as the host of this grand party last night, I would like you to write down on this piece of paper the names of everyone that you can remember who came to your party last. First and last names, and if you did not know a person's family name at least a first name. And next to each name, the nationality if you remember it."

"Mrs. Bonny, could I ask you to do the same thing. Make a list of all those who attended the party last night. Maybe I could ask you to start your list with the people who came to the party and are no longer here. Don't consult with Ken. Give me your list when you're done."

Both started writing right away. Ken felt that Adil was condescending to him and treating him like his teachers had in school days. He also saw right away that Adil was looking to trap the pair in an omission.

A short while later there was a knock on the door. One of Adil's officers opened the door—that is when Bonny realized that that officer had been posted at the door to block anyone from leaving or entering without Adil's permission—and there was the tall figure of Husni, their doorman, in his typically brown Egyptian long robe called the galabiya. He entered the apartment almost apologetically.

"Come in, come in Husni. I want to talk to you some more, following our morning interview." said Adil in Arabic. "Now you told me about the various carloads of guests who came last night for this party in this apartment, but I'd like you to tell me again about the guests that left the party."

"Did you see anyone leave the party and drive away from the building after one in the morning?"

"Oh, I don't know, your Honor. I'm not so sure of the time. I saw two afrangi leave separately at about one o'clock. I told you that. But they left at different times, not together. And just at one o'clock there was a couple who left by car. They got into a car, one of the cars driven by Eritreans. As I said earlier there was a local couple, Dr. Professor Khalid, and his wife who left before midnight. He is Saudi, but he drove himself."

"And you say the big white Porsche that is still there, did not have a driver? That some Saudis arrived in that car—driving themselves—and they carried in some cartons from the back of the car. You even helped carry one of the cartons."

"Yes. They carried the cartons. I carried up one carton. They were bottles."

"How did you know that?"

"They were heavy, filled with liquid. From the way they clinked."

"But that was early in the evening. And these people, three of them, did not leave later?"

"Yeah. They did not leave."

"But there are only two of them here now. So a third must have left during the night and you did not see him?" said Adil harshly.

"Nope I didn't."

"And you didn't see anything fall from the apartment at around the time of the call to Dawn prayer?"

"Nah."

"And you didn't see anyone leave by car in those first minutes of dawn?"

"Nope."

"Because you were asleep, right?"

"Probably."

"Okay Husni, you may go. I'm expecting some vans and vehicles to come here soon. You can show these people how to get up here, okay?"

"Yes, your Honor. Mr. Colonel, sir." And Husni left a little dejected. Adil was annoyed by Husni's groveling manner. He knew that Husni had completely failed in his duties to keep an eye on the door and on the comings and goings of people into and out of the building. And he knew that Husni knew that he had failed, because he had fallen asleep. His negligence had allowed a criminal to get away with murder. Husni would have to pay the price for his negligence. He'd ship him back to Egypt as soon as he took care of all the other crimes committed here at last night's party.

One of his officers came out of the kitchen and signaled to Adil with his hand. Adil walked over to him. The officer said to him in Arabic, "There's something here that you need to see." And then he led Adil out of the big room into the kitchen and then to a utilities corridor in the back of the apartment. He pointed to three unmarked cardboard cartons, all empty. "But look at this one." Without touching the it, Adil looked inside the carton. There were twelve bottles of unopened cabernet wine.

"They brought four cartons in for the party. Three of wine and one of whiskey." Adil said have to himself, half to his investigator. "Maybe they were expecting more people to attend and to drink more. I wonder where Adnan got so much alcohol?" Then out loud he told the shurta officer to try and take fingerprints on the carton. The officer nodded.

When Adil got back to the living room, "his girls" were busy swabbing the inner cheeks of the party guests. Adil could tell, just from the way that everyone was twitching, that they were now getting anxious and impatient.

"Just a little while longer before we move to our next set of tests."

Ken put down the pen and offered Adil the paper where he had made a list of the party attendees.

"Thank you, Dr. Ken. Mrs. Bonny do you have something for me yet?"

Bonny shook her head in the negative and continued. The effort seemed a difficult challenge for her. Adil thought she was really suffering from a hangover.

"You know, I said already that I didn't know all the people who attended." she said, still trying to add one last name to her list. Finally she put down her pen and gave up trying. "Here you are. That's all I can recall."

Adil didn't look at either list right then. Instead he folded them together and put them in a briefcase that was on the floor by the main entry door. He then walked back over and stood over Adnan. In Arabic he sternly addressed Adnan.

"Will you tell us where you got the wine and whiskey?" Adnan didn't even look at Adil. "Does you sister know? Will we have to use harsh measures to force her to speak?"

"Fine, then. Did you bring the hashish, or did Saif Muhammad? What is Saif 's family name?

Anan still refused to answer.

Adil walked over to the dining table and sat down and poured himself some water in a plastic cup. It was still stuffy in the big room. The AC certainly couldn't handle so many people in the room, he thought. There was a knock at the main entry door. The officer guarding it opened the door and admitted two women, dressed as nurses in white uniforms, each carrying four boxes. Behind them Husni brought another six boxes which he set down on the floor next to where the nurses had set theirs down. Touching the top of his forehead and making a slight bow as if in obeisance, Husni backed out of the room and the guard closed the door behind him.

From the color of their skin, and the shape of their faces made it clear that they were Arab, maybe even Saudi, and not Philippinas as most nurses in the Kingdom were. A few years earlier Adil had sent the two women to the U.S. to get specialized training in the SANE forensic program and in how to use the SAFE kits for testing for rape and identifying rapists. It had been difficult to get permission for that—two women traveling by themselves—but in the end Adil had prevailed saying it was an issue of the utmost importance, especially as more and more domestic maids—again Philippinas and Sri Lankans—were coming forward and filing complaints against their Saudi employers for rape. It was his department that had to investigate the claims. It was no longer acceptable to respond by accusing them of adultery and executing them. There were just too many cases. His success was one of the innovations he had successfully introduced in the field of criminal investigation. The kinds of innovations that his sponsors had wanted when they sent him to the U.S. for advanced police methods training. The boxes they had put on the floor were the SAFE kits, for forensic examination of women victims, and in the case of this big party, for female adulterers. Adil considered it an especial prize that both of these women came back from their year in the U.S. speaking fluent English, which was especially helpful in dealing with traumatized Philippinas. He had kept them busy, but their regular job was working in the hospital.

He explained to them in Arabic what the task was on this morning, they were looking around the room at the women especially. They both reacted with some surprise on their faces. They had never done testing of so many foreign women at one time before, with the likely charge of adultery being the primary reason for the tests. They were looking for semen and the semen would be tested for DNA profiles. He said that they could face some serious resistance, especially from Khadija, and that Na'ima and Sabiha could help out if some of the women resisted violently. He told the nurses that he expected that all of the women would claim that they had not had sex that night, but most likely all of them had. Adil did a count around the room again. "I see eight women who you will need to test." he told them.

"Jameel. Did you find your resident card and that of your wife?" Adil spoke across the room in Arabic. Jameel said he had them. "Let me see them." Adil said. Jameel stood up and brought the cards over to Adil who looked carefully at both of them.

"Well that's fine. They indicate that you two are legally married and you have the same last names. And yours indicates that you are an intern at the KFC."

"That's right," Jameel said also in Arabic.

"Well then," said Adil switching into English, "we will know where to find you if we need anything more from you. Collect your things and you and Jameela can now leave. I suggest you go home. Don't talk to anyone at the hospital about the party please. I'm sorry that I have detained you both for such a long time. Not a very nice way to end a party, eh?"

Jameel nodded his head in agreement and rushed back over to his wife. And they picked up what little they had brought with them and started to the door. Then Jameel said to Adil, "We need to take Jameela's abaya. It's in the guest room I think."

Adil nodded and told one of the shurta officers to bring all the abaya's out of the guest room and put them on a sofa. As soon as he did this, Jameela searched through the big pile of black abayas and found one she thought was hers, then the couple left without looking back at anyone in the room.

At the same moment when they left the room, Husni was standing at the door on the landing. He shouted to Adil. "Your honor, the vans have come. Do you need the drivers and guards to come up now?" "No, Husni. In a little while."

"Now, if I could invite the nine remaining women to go with the nurses here to the guest room. The nurses will explain what the next test involves. Don't be worried. Nothing hurts, and it is a test that is over in a flash, if you are cooperative. These are very experienced nurses."

The four Danish women almost jumped up at once as if they were eager volunteers and started to file over to the open door of the guest bedroom. Khajida did not move, nor did Sunithra. Bonny reluctantly stood up. "Don't you need a warrant to be able to take internal probes or such bodily searches?" she said unsteadily. Allison had much the same reaction, but she did not speak out loud and she did not advance to the room. Emily stood up and asked, "You can't do this. I insist on getting a lawyer."

"I won't do anything," Adil answered calmly. "We have every right to carry on these tests because you will be charged with committing very serious crimes. Perhaps the evidence collected will rescind the charges. Now please go to the room and cooperate with the nurses. Fatima and Majda are very good. Ahmad, could you escort Emily to the room?" Ahmad stepped over and motioned to Emily to move in that direction. She moved with obvious reluctance.

Now Bonny felt emboldened. "You have no right. Not to come into my house and conduct bodily searches without my consent."

"Mrs. Bonny. If you don't cooperate, we will have to forcibly collect our sample. And the men will do it. I think with a heavier touch."

Now Bonny was looking at Adil with fire spitting out of her eyes, and her jaws clenched. She walked over and then Allison also walked to the room.

Sunithra did not understand what was going on and she remained seated. "Sunithra, you need to go to the guest room and wait there. No one is going to hurt you. Or Mathandra." Sunithra looked scared but she stood up (she had been sitting on the floor) and walked into the guest room.

"Now Khadija, it is your turn." Adil said in Arabic in a stern voice.

"I won't move, I won't cooperate with your testing." Khadija said. "I want to call a lawyer to come here. I want to call my father."

"A lawyer won't help you in this case. And in any case I won't admit him in here. He can only see you after you get in your jail cell. At the jail they will undress you—completely—and give you a blue jail uniform, and you won't get to keep your lacy underwear. We can extract the semen then forcibly, if we have to, and frankly there is nothing your father can do to stop us. Maybe you will find that less embarrassing, but I can assure that process will be a lot more rough and uncomfortable to you. And I can't guarantee you that you'll have any privacy from other women's or even men's eyes while they conduct that search. They will also look up your anus. Routine really, looking for narcotics. So the choice is yours."

"Do you want us to carry you into the room?"

Khadija, who now looked abject and like a professional keener at a funeral—the kohl around her eyes having melted down her face— looked around the room, and then at her brother. Finally she stood up and moved toward the room. She batted away the arm of one of the officers who offered to help her.

Ken couldn't help think this was all grand theatre to no effect. Sure, Adil could get his nurses training on how to extract vaginal samples. That was easy. But then those samples would surely be ruined, if not lost, in the laboratories where they were sure not to have the qualified lab specialists available to conduct the difficult tests. He had seen that all the time with results that had come from KFC's lab. Incompetence and lack of professional conduct, contaminated samples, botched test results. He used to joke with his colleagues that he didn't think there was a Saudi in the entire kingdom who knew which end of the microscope to put his eyes to.

"You think all of this sample taking will result in accurate, usable DNA profiles?" Ken said snidely to Adil. "You're just fooling yourself that you have a laboratory that can find DNA sequences. And then you still have to match DNA profiles. You probably can't do that either."

"Alas, Dr. Ken. You are right. But we don't use our laboratory—which is still being set up—nor do we use the laboratory at your KFC hospital either. We send our samples out on non-stop refrigerated compartments on jets for testing and analysis at highly qualified forensic crime laboratories in France or the U.S. We've had excellent results over the past three years of running this program. We get results in less than a week. Don't worry about either your wife of your Danish Miss. We'll find out who's been screwing them over the past twelve hours or so."

"Excuse me, no one has been screwing Bonny."

"So you think. We'll find out what she does while you're doing it to your mistress in front of all your guests." Ken shut up. Everyone in the room was looking at him, as if in accusation.

Meanwhile Fatima had told all the women what to expect and how they would proceed. They would examine each woman privately, one by one, and they would take bodily fluids from the vagina and loose pubic hair and that was all. No one would have to completely undress. Majda, with the assistance of Sabiha, would examine four of the women in the guestroom, and the rest would go upstairs where she would do the exams with Na'ima's assistance. She asked those not getting tested to wait just outside the door.

Bonny was to be first. She suddenly had a momentary thought which greatly relieved her anxiety. Since Walt had begged off making love to her that night, she was in no threat of adultery charges. She had been furious when he first said that he couldn't that night. That stupid excuse—saying that he could never get erect after smoking strong pot—had just sent her off. She had so much wanted to show Ken that she had lovers too. She was desperate for some good sex and the party was the best opportunity she had had in months. Walt had always been accommodating before, and sometimes even affectionate. But he was positively strange last night. The exam took three minutes and she got up off the sheet they had spread on the bed and walked back out to the room. She marched over to the table and took a cup and spooned herself out some of the warm sangria, looking at Adil mockingly, defiantly.

In no time the exams were completed until only Khadija and Sunithra were left, and all the other women had come back to the big room and sat down again. As these exams were being carried out, one of the forensic officers came down to the big room carrying a plastic bag in his hand. He whispered something in Adil's ear. Adil answered him in Arabic: "In which room?" The officer told him and Adil gave a little chuckle. "Okay put it in our samples box and label it Khadija's lover." The plastic bag contained a used condom. Apparently Khadija's man was very considerate and didn't want to impregnate her. Instead, thought Adil, he had incriminated her and himself in a most compelling way. Proof was rarely so easily collected. Now all that was left to him was to identify who the young man was that had had sex with Khadija and then ran off while she was sleeping.

Adil walked over to the guestroom where Khadija was still waiting outside for her turn. He knocked gently and waited. After a minute, Majda cracked the door open a little bit. Adil looked away and said to her in Arabic, loud enough so that only Khadija could also hear him. "You don't have to examine Khadija." Then Adil walked back to the dining table and sat down. Khadija looked at him in dismay and then also returned to where she had been sitting. A few minutes later Emily came down the stairs sobbing as she came. She went over to a sofa that was free and sat down, far from Subhi.

"Listen up, everybody." Said Adil, almost as if he were a camp director leading children around. "I am putting you all under arrest and we are going to in twenty minutes load you up on the buses outside and take you to jail, the women will go to the women's jail in al-Bahi district, and the men to the main men's temporary prison in al-Mina district. These will be where you will stay until we can file charges and a trial can be held for each of you. You'll be informed of the charges later. I suggest that in the twenty minutes remaining here that you perhaps wash your faces and use the toilets, drink some water, and for those of you with mobile phones that you call your employer or your national consul to inform them of your change in status."

The people in the room reacted in horror. "You can't do that." one shouted. "Why?" "What charges are you going to hold us on?" another shouted. "I have to call a lawyer." Some of the men stood up and shook their fists at Adil.

Dr. Ken was aghast. This upstart not only barged into his home and without warrants did personal, bodily searches as well as scoured the apartment, but now he was arresting everybody without telling them the charges. After some moments of being transfixed in dismay, he took out his mobile phone and thought to call Her Majesty's Consul in Jeddah; the number he had long ago recorded in his phone, never expecting to need to use it. But he paused before completing the call.

"To arrest us all, don't you have to tell us what you are charging us with?" Ken shouted at Adil.

Adil turned his head to him, smiled again his sarcastic smile and said simply, "No." He thought to counter Ken by saying, 'I suppose you're going to tell me how to administer the law here in Saudi?' but he didn't.

Alison shouted out, "I have diplomatic immunity. You can't take me to jail. Listen to me. I work in the American consul's office here."

"Don't worry, Miss Alison." answered Adil. "That means you'll be the first to be freed. But you should call your office now."

"Time is passing." Adil continued looking relaxed and calm. "You should use the facilities while you can. They won't be so nice in jail."

Hamid came down the stairs and went over and whispered in Adil's ear. "We've found four and half bottles—500 mililiters each—of ethyl alcohol in the distillery bathroom. They each have labels saying they are the property of the King Fahd Hospital and they are not to be used for personal consumption."

Adil looked over at Ken with a look of mock surprise on his face. "And Dr. Ken, in addition to the other serious charges we're going to bring against you, we need to add the theft of alcohol from the hospital where you work. For your distillery no doubt. How could you, Dr. Ken?"

"I didn't steal any of that alcohol. I bought it."

"It's hard to believe. I can't imagine that the hospital can produce a sales invoice to prove your purchase."

Ken fell silent for several minutes, then whispered under his breath, "Bastard". Then he called his Consul. He reached the receptionist and Ken told her the circumstances: a British citizen in trouble with the law and bound for the prison in al-Mina. He asked to speak to the Consul General himself, whom he knew socially, but the receptionist said that he could not speak to him at that time as he was unavailable. She transferred his call to Dennis Watson, a vice consul. Dennis introduced himself and took details from Ken about his arrest and where he would be held, and about his employer. When Ken was finished giving him this information, Watson assured him that he would come visit him in the prison if not tomorrow then that very week. Almost as an afterthought, Ken said, "Oh yes, and my wife Bonny is also being arrested and will be transported to the women's jail in al-Bahi district. Could you visit her also?" Watson said he would and then signed off.

The other people in the group, mostly women, were using the toilets or drinking water. Bonny called the personnel officer at the hospital and told him that she and five nurses would not be coming to work that day or for the near future as they were under arrest. Alison came over to Ken and asked if she could use his mobile phone for a call. Ken looked at her as if this was the strangest request he had ever heard, but then he offered it up. "Yes, and why not?" Alison called her office in the consulate and told them that she was being wrongfully arrested and could they help get her out of jail. Then she handed the handset back to Ken. Adnan was shouting in Arabic rapidly into his mobile phone. Khadija was fretting and pacing in a small circle not far from Adnan. Both were thinking, and hoping, that their father could free them from this nightmare. Adnan was thinking that none of this would have happened if that English bastard had not thrown that Danish girl off the balcony. He was cursing him under his breath, and hoping he would drown at sea.

Finally the time came and Adil announced for the whole room to hear, "Alright, women first. Please take up your abayas. Mrs. Bonny, could you leave with me your keys to this apartment?" The nine women went over to the black pile and started sorting through the abayas. Only Khadija's was easy to recognize as it had elaborate, lacy black embroidery on it. But soon they had distributed the other eight abayas and began to put them on. Bonny meanwhile had found her purse and after a little rummaging through it found her keys. She gave Adil the entire keychain.

"Fine, now girls, Na'ima and Sabiha will lead you down to and onto the bus." The women filed out one by one. Only Sunithra demonstrated any affection and concern in parting from her man, but Sabiha pulled her away from him and she let out a series of little screams and chirping barks as she lost contact with Mathandra's hand. Emily by contrast had already turned her back on Subhi and ignored him as she left. She had called her parents, who had been completely confounded about what to do for their daughter.

Bonny's headache had subsided some from the tablets she had taken earlier. But when she stepped out into the full blaze of the sun falling on the top of her black abaya she was again overcome with the pain and suffering of a hard hangover. She had not looked at or addressed Ken. He was a son of a bitch, she thought he could go to hell. She should have divorced him long ago, she thought, as she stepped into the van. She began to feel more and more bitter against Ken as the van rolled away from Number 11. She didn't even notice Emily sitting next to her, crying.

"And Dr. Ken, if I could have your keys also." said Adil. "And by the way, do you happen to know the name of your landlord here?"

Ken thought for while and then suddenly remembered. It was Sa'ud Muhammad al-Faizi whose office was in the old commercial center of Jeddah. "Why do you need his name?"

"I'm going to tell him he needs to get a more reliable doorman."

Forensic investigations and interrogations

On Thursday, the first of May, Adil met in his air-conditioned office with Ismail al-Thimami, his deputy, Samir Muhsin, the head of the forensics laboratory, and Ibrahim Makarram, the criminal pathologist who ran autopsies. The latter two were Egyptians who both had specialized degrees from Cairo in their line of work. Adil wanted a status report on the investigation into both the Danish girl's death and the "Debauchery Party" as Adil had dubbed the investigations for those thirteen people he had arrested on Sunday.

He wanted to hear Ibrahim Makarram's report first.

"I was able to recover fingerprints from the victim's body, as well as semen samples from both on the vulva and inside the victim's vagina. We also were able to recover skin residues from under her fingernails. She scratched someone's back or shoulders hard. We also recovered some man's pubic hairs—reddish in color. We have prepared all these samples and have given them to Samir to send on to France for DNA profiling. Your investigators did not find any of the victim's fingerprints on the balcony or anywhere else except for a wine glass which was inside the apartment."

"As I said earlier our testing of her blood showed that she was very drunk, if not unconscious at the time. For her body mass and the level of alcohol in her blood, she had probably ten or eleven units of alcohol. She was a big girl, 1.79 tall and 73 kilograms. To have so much alcohol in her blood stream she must have been accustomed to heavy drinking.

The level we found could have killed most average females. But alcohol poisoning did not kill our victim here."

He continued: "There were no signs that she was violently raped or forced entry on her genitals. And there were no bruises on her body, indicating that she was beaten or strangled before her fall."

"What do you put as the cause of Anna's death?" asked Adil.

"When she fell, she was probably still alive, although possibly unconscious from the alcohol. The most probable cause of death was that one of the sharp prongs on the fence severed her spinal cord in the lower thoracic spine. She was impaled in three places altogether. It seems to me just the shock of impact on the prongs was enough to cause death. She probably fell around 3:30-4:00 in the morning, not earlier, and the police agent that first reported her at 5:35 indicated that she was already dead by then. Shock can kill in less time than that. There were no maggots appearing yet from her wounds when the body was discovered, so that indicates to us that she was on the fence at most two hours."

"In fact, now we're no closer to understanding how she fell onto that fence." said Adil, still somewhat frustrated by that conclusion. "She could have been dumped over the railing. In which case, murder. She could have fallen on her own, leaning over the railing to wave goodbye to her lover who had rushed off; in which case accident. She could have fallen over the railing in the act of sex, the pushing from her male partner—the prints taken from the railing and the samples collected from the cushion pushed against the barrier wall are inconclusive. But that would also be accidental. Or in a drunken stupor she could have jumped. Then we have suicide, but I am skeptical of that. And you said, Ibrahim, that it was not most probable that she had already died or was comatose from alcohol poisoning before she fell or was thrown from the balcony. In all cases here we assume that the semen was of one man, and the one man who was most probably involved in her death, either accidental or deliberate. The case of another man seeing her unconscious and raping her after her first lover had left her passed out on the couch, I think, is highly speculative. I think we should rule it out, unless the semen tests show otherwise."

"And until we get those test results back from the French, we are still in the dark about that unidentified man. Probably the redheaded man in the yellow and black checked shirt."

Ismail, Adil's deputy, now broke in. "And the lists of attendees don't tell us who that unknown man was either. We might get a DNA profile back on the man, but we still will not know who it was. We've picked up the two other men on the lists the Addisons left us and we've tested them. If there is a match there, we could have our man."

Adil turned to Samir. "What have you completed so far?"

"As you know we still don't have the capability of doing DNA profiling here in our lab. I prepared all the samples and swabs that were taken from the scene of the party, including the ones that Ibrahim gave me from the victim. We sent them off by courier to France yesterday. The criminal lab there has been very good up to now. We should get the computerized profiles and results back in about two weeks. Unless there are strikes in France."

Ismail cut in apropos nothing at all, "But what I can't get over in this affair is that we had Danish nurses in the country. Only three years after the cartoons scandal in Denmark, how could the hospital been allowed to hire five Danish nurses. Shouldn't they still have been banned?"

"So you think, Ismail, that if there hadn't been Danish girls at that party we would not have had this death and we would not have discovered all these other crimes, adultery especially? If there had instead been five Philippina nurses at this party, we would not have to investigate all these crimes today?" Adil asked Ismail in disbelief. He had often thought that Ismail was more than just a little dim, and he had sometimes wondered how Ismail had been promoted to the level he was at. Must be through family connections, although he had never been able to find what connections had helped Ismail's career.

"Philippinas only have sex with other Philippinos. We've seen that." said Ismail defensively.

"Except when they're raped by their employers." Adil answer annoyed. "Most of our forensic works seemed to go to examining rape cases."

"Yes, of course. Most of our murder cases are solved by bargaining between the families of the accused and the victim. No forensic work needed there."

"We still need the forensics lab here." replied Adil. "Bonny Addison's list included one man who had left the party early. We picked him up at his place of work on Tuesday and were able to take his DNA swabs and fingerprints. There was another man on Dr. Ken's list but not on Bonny's. He also left the party early. It was a strange omission on Bonny's list, because this man, Walter Semms, identified himself as a good friend of Bonny's. Maybe there was a reason that Bonny wanted to hide his identity?"

"And maybe there is some reason that both of them are hiding the unidentified killer?" answered Ismail in a sarcastic tone.

"Yes, of course. I myself suspect that Dr. Ken is for some reason or other hiding that man's identity." said Adil. "I suppose I should interrogate both of the Addison's. Maybe next week. I could use their omissions against both of them. Their consulate is asking for their release on bail. But I think we won't do that. I think we can coerce them to reveal the name of our unknown killer by letting stay and sweat in isolation in their prison cells. In Dr. Ken's case we have other very serious charges against him, and we can perhaps negotiate with him some relief from those charges in return for cooperation in identifying the killer, and where he might be."

"You mean a heavy caning instead of a beheading for his adultery?" asked Ismail.

"Yes, that is exactly what I mean. But we have to get the message across to him that that is what he is facing. I'm pretty sure once he realizes he'll lose his head if he doesn't cooperate, then maybe he'll change his mind."

Adil pulled out a pack of Marlboro's and knocked two cigarettes out of the pack. He offered the second one to Ismail. He knew already that his Egyptian assistants did not smoke cigarettes, only occasionally smoking a waterpipe. He lighted his and Ismail's cigarette. And then the idea struck him again.

"Samir, did you get any DNA off that small remains of a joint that we recovered from the balcony?" Adil asked as he puffed out smoke.

"Yes, actually." said Samir. "We were able to get a good lip print and we were able to recover what looked like residual DNA material from the paper. We sent it off with the other samples. And I think we will compare the DNA profile from that we took from the swabs we have taken from this Mr. Childer and Mr. Simms after their arrest."

"And what about the car? Did our men recover any other hashish from Adnan's car?"

"Yes, both ash and loose particles of hashish. They were found in the rear seat ashtray. The loose particles tested as coming from the same batch as that which was found on the balcony at Number 11."

"And any fingerprints from the rear seat?" asked Adil as he stubbed out his cigarette.

"We got several different sets of fingerprints. One was a set that belongs to Khadija. One print was Adnan's. But we also got prints of several fingers which don't belong to either of those two. On the night of the party there was a third person in the rear seat of the car?"

"Yes we know that. But we don't know the name of the individual there."

"We'll have to squeeze this guy, Walter Semms." said Ismail. "We have testimony that he smoked on the balcony with this unknown hash-head. And we could put the squeeze on Khadija too."

"I was already thinking of that." Adil replied. "There was one unidentified man on Dr. Ken's list, named Saif. We'll try to find out more about who this Saif is and whether or not he is the hash-head."

The group fell silent. Finally Ibrahim broke the silence as he wanted to leave.

"We have completed the embalming of the Danish woman's body and have now put her in the deep freeze. Has someone contacted her parents about disposing of her body?"

Adil replied calmly. "Yes, we started anyway. My men went to the hospital and got the contact numbers of the agency that recruited her here from Denmark. They gave these numbers to the Foreign Office and they said they would be taking care of it. But I can imagine that they are in no hurry. So you'll have to keep her for a while. But she is prepared for repatriation, right?"

"Yes."

And with that the meeting broke up.

The next day Colonel Adil had Walter Semms brought before him in an interrogation room next to his office. He was surprised to see a tall, late middle-aged man with graying hair. Semms appeared to be English by his passport, but when Adil tried to confirm this, he corrected Adil and said he was Welsh.

"I imagine, Mr. Semms, that you want to know why we have arrested you and are holding you?"

"Yes, I have done nothing wrong."

"No, that is not exactly right. You went to that party last week at Dr. Ken Addison's apartment, or should I say orgy? And you drank and smoke pot. And we would like to know who you fucked at the party."

"I didn't have sex with anyone there that night." said Semms.

"You mean you didn't bring that American girl, Alison, along with you for a little sex and fun?"

"No, no. I just gave her a ride. I know her from the choir that I direct."

"Okay, and doesn't Mrs. Bonny Addison also sing in your choir?

"Yes, that's how I knew about the party. She invited me."

"So you went to have sex with her?"

"No, Bonny and I are just good friends." He lied, they were in fact lovers and had been having sex after choir practice at his house for a few months already.

"Well, do you know that she brought a number of Danish nurses from her hospital to provide sexual services to the other male guests? Did you participate?"

"No, I didn't. And she did not bring them for that purpose. She just invited them for some social activity and fun."

"I see. But did you also know that after you left there was a murder at that party and that one of the Danish girls was killed, on the same balcony where you and a few others earlier had gone to smoke pot?"

"No, I didn't know that. That's terrible news."

"Yes, terrible especially for Anna—that was the victim's name. You didn't happen to have sex with her before she met her terrible fate?"

"No. I left the party early, around one o'clock. I told the interrogators about that, already."

"Did you see this Anna, tall, blond, slender, with a heavy man with red curly hair and wearing a yellow and black checked shirt?"

"I may have. But I didn't know Anna. And I am not sure I remember seeing any man like what you just described. Not with any of the Danish girls."

"You don't deny smoking pot on the balcony?"

"No."

"With Adnan and a certain man named Saif?"

"Yes. Adnan is well known. But I didn't know this man named Saif. I think he said his name was Saif Ahmad. Adnan said he worked with him and that he had the best marijuana in the Kingdom. We smoked a few joints together and then I went back into the party."

"Where does Adnan work? I thought he worked in his father's bank."

"No, Adnan runs a trading firm. In the old city. But it may be that his father owns the trading company."

"So you deny having sex with any of the women at the party that night. Be careful we have tested all of the women and if you had we will find out."

"No. I didn't. Absolutely deny that. It was strong marijuana and I left early because after smoking that I was not feeling particularly well."

"Fine, well back to the jail cell for you. You'll probably be taken to trial within the month. But if you remember something important before then, something you want to tell me, let the warden know."

That was easy, thought Adil, as Semms was led away. Adil went back to his office and ordered that a team go over to Adnan's trading company—they had already identified it—and arrest one Saif Ahmad. Maybe one of their trade items was illegally imported hashish. Along with the wine and whiskey.

But the next morning, the team found that Saif Ahmad was not at the trading house. There was a Bengali clerk there who was actually in the process of locking up the firm when they arrived. He identified Saif Ahmad al-Janbari as an employee and a friend of Adnan's. But that he had not come to the offices since the last Sunday in April and he not either been in touch. He himself was closing the office because Adnan had been arrested and Saif had disappeared and there was no one left to manage the office or conduct business. When asked if that business was the import of wine, whiskey and hashish, the Bengali clerk's eyes grew wide in horror. "Oh no, sir, we don't do any illicit trade. Nothing like that. I assure you." The Bengali had to open up the office to find if they had an address for Saif. All he could find though was a personal account number where he regularly made salary payments to Saif: an account in the NBH, the bank of Adnan's father.

And the search for Saif Ahmad continued. The next day Adil sent an investigator to the bank with a request to get the home address of the holder of the account. It took the bank some time to agree to disclose this, but by noon they had matched the account number to the client's data and they gave to the investigator Saif Ahmad's home address. That same afternoon, a team went to Saif Ahmad's apartment. He was not in and his wife did not know where he had absconded to for the previous week. Adil decided to put the house under surveillance and to wait for Saif—who had clearly gone into hiding—to come back. After five days, the watchman spotted Saif sneaking into his house early in the morning. He called for help and a team went out and found him and arrested him. He had gone into hiding, but had not gone far at all. Only to his tribal home near Najran but he had needed to tell his wife and get some changes of clothes. Later, when Adil began to interrogate Saif Ahmad, he got the same kind of response that Adnan had given him, sullen silence. He wouldn't say where he had obtained the hashish, where the cartons of wine had come from and how Adnan had gotten them, and he shrugged off knowing anything about the heavyset man in a yellow and black checked shirt at the party. Adil sent him back to his jail cell. This was going to require much more persuasive methods, thought Adil, and by that he meant torture and deprival. If he needed to wait to twist or burn an answer out of Saif, he could do that.

The next day after that interrogation, Adil sent Ismail to the trading company to question the Bengali clerk about Saif Ahmad's activities. The store front was still locked up with steel folding shutters drawn over the front wall. But when Ismail the telephone numbers on the store front, one of them was answered by the Bengali. Ismail told what he wanted to ask him about, and the Bengali man agreed to come to the store and open it up to tell him what he could about Saif Ahmad. From his questioning it emerged that Saif Ahmad had over the previous year and a half had flown to Addis Ababa in Ethiopia every three weeks without fail supposedly on company business. The Bengali clerk said he had always thought this was strange because he went to Addis for only two days, and he always said it was to buy coffee to import. But in all the time that Saif was doing this, they had received only one small consignment of coffee, even though every trip he claimed expenses of several thousands of dollars for the purchase of something said to be coffee on the invoices. Ismail asked if Saif could have been buying and smuggling in narcotics on these trips. Again the Bengali clerk denied this vehemently, saying he never saw any narcotics and they did not import any either. But Ismail nevertheless concluded that that was just what Saif was doing in Addis every month, buying hashish and somehow bringing it back with his luggage. Ismail looked at the invoices and found that all of them were signed by a man named Jameson Piper, a mysterious English name and not an Ethiopian one. The invoices also had the address of a firm in Shashamene, not in Addis. That was the place in Ethiopia where hashish was grown, he knew. Ismail was sure that this Mr. Piper was selling hashish to Saif and not coffee. And Adil concurred. They just did not know how Saif Ahmad smuggled the hashish into the Kingdom.

Meanwhile back in May on the next day after their first strategy meeting to discuss progress, Adil and two other officers went in the early evening—a time when it was still light but the summer heat was usually beginning to recede—to the registered address of Dr. Ismail Mansur and his wife Mishal. Dr Ismail answered the door and Adil introduced himself and asked to be let it to ask him a few questions concerning the party. When he took a seat in the front sitting room, first of all he wanted to know if Dr Ismail knew about the arrests that followed the party, mainly for adultery, but also for general debauchery, drunkenness and smoking hashish. Dr. Ismail called for his wife Mishal to join them. "She was at the party with you?" asked Adil. "Yes, or course." "And how do you know Dr. Addison and his wife Bonny?"

"Oh, I work as an anesthesiologist at the KFC with Dr. Addison. Know him exceedingly well." Said Dr Ismail who it turned out spoke with an English accent but with south Asian speaking patterns and stresses, including a slight wobbling of his head. His passport showed that he was an English citizen of Pakistani origin, as was his wife and they had both been working in the kingdom for four years. "We have gone to a few of their parties."

"Did you or your wife drink while you were there?"

"Well, you know, I think I might have had a nip." Dr Ismail said while smiling nervously. "Nothing much. But Mishal not anything other than juice."

"But you are Muslim, aren't you?"

"Yes."

"And you know it is forbidden to drink alcohol."

"Well yes. But actually, my dear man, in the discussion of the law it is forbidden to be drunk, but not to drink. Of course, drinking alcohol does tend to cause drunkenness, but what I drank certainly doesn't."

"So how much do you think you drank?"

"Of wine? Maybe 15 milliliters just to appear sociable. Nothing else. No whisky or punch."

"Did you know that the party turned in rather what you could call an orgy after the drinking and music and dancing?"

"No. But we left early just as the dancing started."

"And what time was that?"

"Just after eleven thirty."

"Do you think anyone can corroborate that?"

"Oh yes, our driver for one can corroborate that we left early."

"And did you know that later in the night, a young woman at the party was possibly raped and killed."

Dr. Ismail and Mishal reacted with fright and shock. "My dear God, no we did not know."

"And the victim was one of the Danish nurses from your hospital who had been brought to the party by Mrs. Bonny. Did you know that?"

"No that is horrible news. Oh the poor dear girl. I know some of the Danish nurses, but I had not suspected that one of their number was killed at the same party where we were. I have noticed that many of the Danish nurses have disappeared from the hospital."

"That's because we are holding them in prison on charges of adultery and indecency."

"Oh, Allah help us. What has transpired? It was such a fun party. Nothing sinful, while we were there."

"Except maybe for erotic party games, and excessive drinking." said Adil sternly.

"But we did not participate in any of that. I can assure you, honorable sir." Dr. Ismail was no longer smiling.

"We still have not found the murderer of the Danish nurse. But we have some suspects. Perhaps you or your wife noticed a heavyset man, a red-headed man in a yellow and black checked shirt at the party. I'm sure he drank. And he probably danced too. Although no one seems to have seen him play the party games."

"We also did not play the party games. Too much touching. Not for us, especially to play with others. I don't touch other women."

"That's the way it should be. As it is commanded. And of course, Mishal does not touch other men."

"Oh Allah save us. No of course not. But as for the heavy man in a yellow shirt, I don't think that I recall seeing him, I certainly don't know such a man if he was there."

"Ismail, shame on you." said Mishal. "We have seen such a man at that party. And I know I have seen someone who sounds like the same man you describe at the Addisons' parties several times before. He looked very familiar this time. It's his curly red hair, dark sunburned neck, as if he works outdoors. He is heavyset as you said, and fairly tall. I think he speaks with a Scottish accent. But I don't know his name, nor do I know if he is from Scotland."

"Thank you, Mrs. Mishal. You're the first to acknowledge this man. He is our prime suspect. Now if we could only put a name to him."

"But surely Dr. Addison knows him by name." said Dr. Ismail. "And should know him well. As Mishal said, this man, he is usually at their parties. Although he has never been introduced to us."

Adil did not like this equivocation in Dr. Ismail.

"And how did you go to the party that night?"

"Why in our car. Our driver, Abdel Aziz drove us there. And brought us back."

"Could I speak to him?"

"Yes, of course. I'll go call him." Said Ismail. Mishal excused herself, but first asked if Colonel Adil or his deputies would like to have some tea. They declined.

It was clear at once to Adil when Abdel Aziz entered the room that he was also a foreign worker. From Africa, no doubt, and from his looks and the shape of his face either from the Horn of Africa or Eritrea or Djibouti. Adil addressed the man in Arabic, and at once it was clear that he was from Eritrea. Adil watched carefully and he was convinced that Dr. Ismail and his wife did not understand Arabic in spite of their four years living in the kingdom.

"Abdel Aziz, tell me, you drove Dr. and Mrs. Mansur to the party there at the end of April?"

"Yes, I did."

"And after you dropped them at the party, what did you do? Did you stay there and wait for them?"

"Yes. I parked the car under the building and waited for them." Abdel Aziz spoke decent Arabic which Adil found surprising as generally the migrant laborers from across the Red Sea had trouble with the language.

"When did they leave the party?"

"Must have been around midnight."

"And what were you doing during those four or five hours that they were at the party?"

"Nothing especially. I talked to one of my mates, also a driver. A guy also from Asmara that I know a bit. His name is Muhammad. He was driving a white Chevy Malibu. Very nice car."

"Who was he driving for?"

"I don't remember what he said exactly. Something about a captain so and so."

"But you had met this Muhammad with the captain's Malibu before?"

"Yes, a couple times before. Usually at Dr. Ken's parties."

"That was not the first time that you saw the captain's driver there?"

"No. As I said, I have driven the Mansurs there a few times before. And Muhammad and I, we always chat together."

"Chew some qat together while you waited?"

"No, nothing illegal like that. He's a good boy. And I don't chew."

"Did you see this captain arrive at the party or leave?"

"No. I did not see who Muhammad drove. He was already there when I brought the Dr. and his missus. And we left before he did."

"Do you know where to find this Muhammad Mansur?"

"No. No idea. Maybe down at the marina?

"Why do say the marina?"

"He told me that the captain was a real captain and he had a big boat down at the marina."

"Thank you, Abdel Aziz, you can go."

Adil turned his attention back to Dr. Ismail and Mishal.

"Something tells me that you are not being entirely honest with me. Lying and equivocating are very serious sins for Muslims, don't you know? You don't know this Captain character, yet he has several times attended parties with you at Dr. Ken's place. How can that be."

"I told the truth. I don't know his name." said Dr. Ismail acting a little sheepish and wagging his head more than usual.

Adil went away from Dr. Ismail's house feeling certain that Dr. Ismail, just like Dr. Ken and Adnan, was hiding something. When he stepped outside, it was already dark. The sun's blaze had gone, but it was still a hot, stuffy and humid night, the heavy air did not move at all from the streets of the city. He appreciated it that his driver had left the car's air conditioner running while he was inside. He settled into the rear seat of his car and thought what to do next. He decided to go to his cousin's evening social divan where they usually talked about politics and smoked cigarettes.

The next morning, Adil himself, with his deputy Ismail, went to the main offices of the National Bank of the Hijaz. He asked the male receptionist who was dressed in a black London tailored suit if he could call Tony Childer to come down to the entrance lobby. The receptionist called a number, and in English requested that the man who answered come right away to the main lobby. "I understand that you may be busy, but this is really urgent. There is a police officer who requires that you come speak to him."

They had to wait five minutes until a young slender man dressed in a summer weight puce colored suited emerged from a bank of elevators and walked calmly over to the entrance gates. He stepped through and addressed the receptionist, who pointed to Adil.

"Yes, so here I am. I am Anthony Childer. You want to speak to me?"

"Good morning Mr. Childer. Do you have your passport with you? You are American, am I right?"

"Yes I am. No, I don't carry my passport with me. The human resources department here holds my passport."

"But you have your residence and work permit with you, don't you?" asked Adil politely.

"Yes, of course. What is this all about?" asked Anthony a little nonplussed.

"We're here to put you under arrest for crimes committed at a party held in the house of Dr. Ken Addison on the night of the 26th to the 27th. Let's have the permit."

"You must be mistaken." said Anthony as he reached for his wallet in his inside jacket pocket. He handed a blue residence permit card, which was the size of a passport, to Adil who briefly eyed it. "I committed no crimes." said Tony. "It was a party in a private house. And I am not Muslim, so I didn't violate any Muslim laws."

"But you also go by the name, Tony?" asked Adil. "Why is that?"

"Oh, it's just the nickname for Anthony. Tony, Antony, Anthony."

"And your father's name is Fredericks?"

"No. That is just a middle name. My father's name is Robin. We don't use patronymics as middle names like you do here. My middle name is my grandmother's family name."

Adil thought once more how strange it was that Westerners didn't use patronymics.

"You confirm that you were at Dr. Ken's party about two weeks ago?"

"Yes. I was there. But I didn't commit any crimes. And I left relatively early."

"Early? Like at eleven o'clock?"

"No. But at two o'clock. When the music was still playing and a few people were still dancing."

"Tell me, Tony, at the party did you recognize a heavy man with curly red hair in a yellow and black checked shirt? Probably dancing with one of the tall Danish nurses."

"No, I don't think so. There were lots of people there I didn't know."

"Do you know that one of the members of the party, a man presumably, killed a Danish woman there?"

"No. First I heard about it. How awful."

Adil looked closely at Tony's expression as he reacted to the news, but he couldn't detect any sign of guilt or evasiveness.

"Who invited you to the party then?" Adil asked.

"Adnan invited me." Tony lied without a moment's hesitation; he did not want to implicate Khadija who had actually invited him to join her at the party. Adil did not pick up on the lie.

"But you came on your own? And not with Adnan, right?"

"That's right. I drove myself."

"Fine. You'll come with me now."

"Where? What do you mean I'll come with you?"

"I told you. I'm arresting you. And now we'll take you straight to the Baji prison."

"Whoa. Can I call someone?"

"Yeah. Make it quick."

"I have to tell my wife. And I should tell the American Consul."

"Go ahead. But tell me. You went to the party with or without your wife?"

"Without."

"Strange, such a sexy erotic party and so much booze and dancing and you didn't take your wife?"

"No. She couldn't go."

Hard to believe, Mr. Tony."

"Well, she couldn't, and she didn't."

Tony made a quick call to his boss at the bank, then he tried to reach the American Consul, but had to leave a message, and finally he called his wife. "I don't know why I'm being arrested, honey. I'm going to prison apparently. Here in Jeddah. Call Max and ask him to help. Yes, I'll probably be out of touch for a long while. Don't worry. Remember what we discussed if I should disappear. You may have to do what we discussed. I love you too. Now don't worry."

"And Mr. Tony, it really doesn't matter that you're not a Muslim. If you violate Sharia law here, you'll be judged and punished by Sharia law. You were probably told that when you first came to this country, and were employed."

Adil then led Tony out of the bank and put him in the back of the police car that Ismail had come in.

Before he stepped into his own car, Adil told Ismail to be sure to get the DNA swab samples from Tony, along with his fingerprints.

In late May, the French lab sent back the results of their DNA profiling of the samples they had collected from the party goers. Early in the morning on Thursday, the end of the work week, Samir came to Adil's office to deliver him a report on DNA profiles of the party-goers. He was excited because they had a lot of perfect matches.

Almost before he could start Adil stopped him. He had a pad of legal size, yellow paper in front of him and he got out his expensive fountain pen—a Waterman pen that his boss had awarded him for excellent performance during an investigation they had done together in England—and began testing it to see that it wasn't clogged. Then he said to Samir: "I know you've prepared your report in a certain way, but let's start with the most important criminal aspect of this party. Tell me first of all was the semen on and inside Anna, our dead victim, from only one man?"

"Yes. The lab confirmed that all the samples we took off of Anna came from the same man. And they gave a good DNA profile too. But they don't belong to any of the men we have tested so far. Thus, whoever had sex with Anna, remains unidentified. Furthermore, the skin residues we recovered under her fingernails also yielded matching DNA profile. The samples which came from the back or shoulders under Anna's nails belong to the same man who deposited his semen on her."

"Good." said Adil. "We can rule out then that another man may have either raped her or thrown her over the balcony after Anna had had passionate sex with this man. And your fingerprint evidence seems to demonstrate that during her passion she was holding onto the railing of the balcony. We're looking for one man and everything points to the red-headed heavy-set man in the yellow and black checked shirt, who was seen by several of our party-goers with Anna during the games and dancing times. And who was seen, at least by Alison, late stepping out onto the balcony with Anna."

Adil wrote down a few notes, then took out his cigarettes and lit one up for himself and offered one to Samir, who declined. "Fine, continue now with your report."

"The lab has prepared DNA profiles of everyone we sampled at the party, including those of Dr. Ismail and his wife Mishal. The samples we collected from, Saif Ahmad al-Janbari, and the foreigners, Walter Semms and Anthony Childer, we only sent last week and we haven't gotten those results back yet. We have them on our computer system and this allows us to compare profiles taken from different sources."

"We also recovered semen from five of the women we tested at the party. But we did not recover any traces of semen from Mrs. Bonny Addison or from Alison Plumper."

Adil chuckled. "I know that Alison is rather plump, but her family name is Plummer. Correct that please."

"Yes sir. I'll change it. I didn't record the names. This was probably a mistake by one of the SANE nurses."

"Well, this means we cannot bring any adultery charges against Mrs. Bonny." muttered Adil. "Rather surprising considering the state of undress I found her in when she first answered the door to me." He thought for a few moments and then said further, "And we'll have to let Alison go altogether. But we can ask the Foreign Ministry to request that she be removed from the Kingdom for participating in a debauchery. Diplomatic immunity or not."

"Then, we identified four men who committed fornication or adultery from their semen in the five women found to have been inseminated. They are: Ken Addison in the Danish woman named Elsa, Adnan son of Abdallah al-Misha'ri in the Danish woman named Agnate, Subhi

Muhammad in the English woman named Emily, and Mathander in the Sri Lankan woman named Sunithra."

"That would mean that we have three cases of adulterous fornication, and one of simple fornication because neither Subhi or Emily are married to others. I think our morality police would have a field day with these results." said Adil.

"And we recovered semen," continued Samir, "from the unmarried woman Khadija daughter of Abdallah al-Misha'ri, but while the lab gave us a DNA profile for that semen sample, we don't have it matching to any of the DNA samples we took. Maybe it will belong to these other men whom we tested later. And we will learn later then."

"Maybe. If God wills it."

"But the lab told us that the DNA profile they produced from this Sri Lankan man is contaminated. Something went wrong in the collection process or in transferring it to the lab. So they can't say with a hundred percent accuracy, or even eighty percent accuracy, that this semen belongs to the Mathander who we tested."

"But the identity of the other three men are high probability of a match? The lab has high confidence that they identified matching DNA profiles?"

"Yes. High degree of probability."

"Good." said Adil. "That means I won't have to pursue vigorously an adultery case against the Sri Lankans. They will be charged of consorting, and sleeping together. But they will not be executed. I feel sorry for these poor domestic servants. They will be whipped and expelled and that will be harsh enough for them."

"So does that mean that you'll pursue adultery charges against the others?"

"Yes. Did the lab in France specify a high probability of accuracy in these other profiles?"

"Yes. They did. A very high degree of confidence. Greater than 95 percent accuracy for a match."

"With that, I think I can press my case." said Adil. "But we still don't have identification of the man who inseminated Khadija, do we?"

"No. But maybe we will learn more in the next batch of results." said Samir. "When we get them back."

"Thanks for all this. Did you find anything else?"

"Yes. You know we found the paper butt of a hashish joint? We were able to take a sample off of it, and the French lab was able to recover enough DNA material that they could do a genetic profile. We got that back but it doesn't match any of the people for whom we have DNA profiles already. So maybe it belongs to Semms, or to Saif Ahmad, or to our unidentified killer."

"Maybe. It would be good to find out. Rather sooner than later. I feel pretty certain our killer has fled the country and the longer he is away the harder it will be to bring him to justice."

When Adil got back to his office. He remembered his interview with Abdal Aziz. He thought to himself that he should investigate the statement the driver had made about a captain and a marina. He decided to send Ismail, but then changed his mind and decided to go himself. But he would have to go the next morning because it was already one o'clock and nearly everyone was finishing with work and heading off to the midday meal.

He went first to the port manager. He asked him if there had been any departures on the morning of the 27th of April from the private yacht marina. The manager called up the records keeper for the port log of that day. This latter came some minutes later with a large folio sized ledger book. He opened it and flipped through the large pages until he came to the 27th. There were six departures from the port that day, all commercial ships. And at the Aramco oil products port there had two been departures of tankers.

"Wait, here's something." said the records keeper. He pointed to the bottom of the page where there was an entry with some blank cells.

"It seems there was an unauthorized, unregistered sailing at five thirty that morning, just after sunrise. You can see we've filled in the information we know. And since it was unauthorized, we didn't know much about the vessel. It was a private yacht for sure. That happens only very rarely. Usually an owner that forgets to fill in the proper papers before departure. But you'll have to check at the marina to find out more."

Adil told his driver to take him to the private yacht marina which was a couple kilometers away. He was glad that his driver had left the car's air conditioning running. It was a very hot and humid morning down by the waterside.

The marina management was less organized than at the port. They did not keep careful detailed records of arrivals and departures because so many of the large yachts were owned by very important people who did not want to have their comings and goings recorded. Adil's question about an unauthorized early morning departure of one of the marina's large yachts on the 27th of April drew no response. "Could have happened. But we can't be sure. We don't have a record of one of our boats leaving then."

Adil thought further. Maybe it was a very big yacht.

"Have any of your very large yachts—seaworthy yachts that could travel to Europe—gone missing from its regular docking space in the past three or more weeks?"

The boat manager who was responsible for supplying utilities and water to the docked ships thought hard for a while. "You understand there are quite a few such seaworthy sized yachts here in recent years."

he said as he thought about it. "But now that you mention it, the Chrysanthemum has been missing from its berth for almost four weeks. It's owned by the bank."

"The bank?" asked Adil.

"Yeah in recent years the NBH, the Hijazi Bank, has been selling yachts to VIPs in the city. The registration remains with the bank to hide the true owners' names, but also because the bank finances the purchases. It's a good business they have. We have lots of Saudi princes who keep yachts here. And some top Aramco bosses too."

"You say, the Chrysanthemum has gone missing for almost a month?"

"Yep."

"But you don't know it's owner?"

"No. Not other than the Bank. The Bank owns most of the big yachts in our marina. But it has a foreign captain who acts as if he were its owner."

"A big red-haired fellow—say almost fat? Looks like he's Scottish or something like that?"

"Yeah. That's the captain. He's exactly that big, heavy, and with curly red hair. He usually wears a captain's cap. I don't know about Scottish or anything like that. I don't speak English. He's a bluff sort. He's been running the boat for the past five or six years. He often sails on foreign trips from here."

"Do you know his family name? This captain?"

"No. Well, maybe. His crews would call him Captain Matt."

Adil concluded he would have to ask at the Bank. Ask after a Captain Matt. Maybe they would tell him.

A week later he went to the women's prison to interview Bonny Addison. She was brought to him in a small, windowless, air-conditioned room. She was wearing shapeless loose light blue pants and a tunic type shirt that fell to below her bottom—they looked like pajamas made of bleached denim. He hair had been cut very short and her face no longer held any traces of make up or cosmetics. Adil noticed that there were heavy beads of sweat on her forehead and even on her nose. She was made to sit on a wooden chair on one side of a table. He sat on the opposite side. Ismail sat with him; even though his English was weak he could understand a lot. Adil had a yellow legal sized pad (he had brought lots of them from the U.S. when he returned from his studies) and he took notes with his prized Waterman fountain pen.

"Mrs. Bonny, there are a few things I would like to ask you, if you don't mind. First, you told us that on the night of the party you did not see a heavy, red-headed man in a yellow and black checked shirt. And yet he was dancing with one of your own Danish nurses. The nurse named Anna—an unforgettable looking woman, tall, white skinned, blond— yet you could not remember seeing her with him. Others saw them dancing together, very intimately, through the party. And Alison saw him step out onto the balcony with her. And yet, you did not include him in your list of attendees. How do you explain that?"

"Am I charged with anything. Why are you holding me in this vile jail? When can I consult with a lawyer?" asked Bonny with a hint of fury in her voice. She finished her questions and immediately took a long drink of water from the glass set out on her side of the table.

"In due time you'll get a lawyer. Have you been visited by your Consul?"

"No. I presume you won't let him visit me."

"Oh no, we can't prevent your government's representative from coming here to see you. Perhaps he doesn't want to see you."

"So, answer my questions then. What am I charged with?"

"It's not for you to ask me questions, Mrs. Bonny. Answer my question and I might answer yours."

"It's easy to answer. I don't know this man. I didn't invite him, and I didn't notice him dancing with Anna. I was dancing with someone else."

"Perhaps you were dancing with Walter Semms? You didn't include him on your list either. But your husband did."

"Bastard." Bonny hissed. "I may have been dancing with Mr. Semms. But I also danced with others." Actually, she thought. she had been dancing exclusively with Walt, intimately and erotically dancing with him, and kissing him, and caressing him as they danced. She had wanted to make love to him, like they had the week before at his place, after choir practice. She tried to conjure up from her memory an image of what Walt's face looked like. But she couldn't. She could only imagine in her mind's eye the moment when she had taken his long penis into her hands and put it into her mouth. But the image was interrupted by Adil's next question.

"Are they treating you well here?"

Bonny looked at Adil with surprise mixed with anger. "Well? What do you mean? That these Amazons here don't starve me, or beat me all the time? This is a filthy overcrowded prison that is hot like an oven. The toilets stink to high heaven. It's not a Club Med resort, you know."

"Of course not. This prison is for punishment."

"Have I been charged with anything? Has the court already judged my case and sentenced me to imprisonment?"

"No, we'll get to that in time. But tell me. Doesn't the name Captain Matt mean anything to you? Don't you recognize it?"

"No."

"Why are lying to me, Mrs. Bonny? Dr Ismail's driver said he was driven your parties on several occasions. This man is a beast and killer. A heartless monster, who was accustomed to coming to your parties. Why do continue to hide his name from me?"

"Why are you holding me? I don't give a damn what a driver told you. I don't know him or recognize that name." She was lying, and she knew it. Captain Matt was the man who usually brought all the wine and liquor for their parties. He was not capable of killing Anna. She knew that for sure.

"I was thinking of charging you with being a procuress for your Danish girls. I think all of them fornicated at your party, and I think they were specially brought to the party for that reason. But they could not have expected to be thrown off your balcony."

"That's a strange charge. Is that a crime in your bloodthirsty Islamic law? I thought a procuress only existed if there was a monetary transaction between a prostitute and a client."

"I don't have to justify anything to you about our sharia. You know that being a procuress is wrong. Even in England it is a crime."

"I would like to speak to my Consul. I demand that you release me, at once. I have nothing more to say to you."

"Well maybe you'll have more to say to the judge."

"That would suit me. He'll let me free."

Adil took out a cigarette and lit it. But he did not say anything. His eyes were boring in on Bonny, looking at her the same way he had when she first opened her door to him only partially dressed, but his expression was not especially vengeful. It seemed to Bonny that he was amused by the situation and Bonny's plight. After he stubbed out his cigarette, Adil stood up and pressed a button on his side of the table.

"I advise you to ask for the mercy of the court. And it will go better for you if you confess to your crime. That's all I have to say, Mrs. Bonny."

The door behind Bonny opened and one of the Amazon wardens came in and took Bonny by the arm. She was trying to think about Walt, but she couldn't. She was still baffled about why he had not wanted to make love to her that last night of her freedom. She lurched back for the water glass and resisted the tugs of the Amazon while she gulped down the last of the water in it.

Judgments are harsher in summertime

True summer begins in Jeddah around the end of April and runs through the end of September. For the first two months, daily temperatures rise to above 40 degrees Celsius and humidity falls as the unclouded sun desiccates the coastal region. There are winds that come down from the northwest over the Red Sea and they can bring some relief from the humidity nearest the shore and near the districts around the port. But these often fail and are replaced by the desiccating north winds that bring mid-summer dust storms into the city—days when the blazing hot sky has the color of concrete dust. These are the summer months when the most powerful air conditioning units run at full blast and the town's people spend almost the entire daytime period indoors. Some people will walk along the old corniche in the late evening twilight on days when the Northwest winds are blowing and temperatures can fall to the mid-thirties. The summer is noted for days and days of unremitting scorching sun that seems to burn through the walls of all buildings and turn many of the concrete residential buildings into ovens. Temperatures run in the upper 40s for almost three months. For many of the city's inhabitants, the high summer is a time, for those who can afford it, to leave Jeddah for summer vacations in cooler climates like the Mediterranean coast, the mountains of Lebanon, or to cities in Europe such as London, Nice, or Rome. They will be gone for two sometimes two and half months. If that time can include Ramadan, the month of fasting, so much the better. It's much easier to fast in milder weather and during shorter days. Most of the western expatriates, who work in high paying jobs in finance, engineering, or medicine, also leave for six weeks in the middle of each summer.

But for those who remain in the city throughout the summer, social life becomes constricted and people are rarely seen on the streets, or in public venues. The most acceptable public space where people gather in the summer are the big flashy shopping malls, which are all well air conditioned. It is as if the city's entire population remaining in place becomes introverted, crankier and short-tempered, moods that reflect the unremitting heat. Judges in the criminal courts, no less than other people in other walks of life, became no less foul tempered and are prone to hand out harsher sentences upon conviction or to postpone cases altogether to the late fall. Adil had over the previous seven years noticed this trend, as had many other prosecutors, although the justice authorities insistently denied that this happened. But even if sentences were not harsher in summertime, the mere postponement of court trials means that jail inmates suffer especially harshly by languishing in prisons for an extra four or five months over the summer months—a punishment that outsiders consider to be one of the most inhumane punishment that Saudi Arabia imposes: indefinite detentions in filthy, un-air-conditioned prisons without charges or scheduling of a hearing in court, often in isolation. Attitudes to this indirect punishment inside Saudi Arabia are unforgiving. For the foreigners and especially foreign migrant laborers so imprisoned, most Saudis feel—if they think about the issue of harsh incarceration at all—that it was no less than what those people deserved.

Adil did not hold that view of extended incarceration to be justified, but he was still somewhat ambivalent about holding people indefinitely without charges in cruel conditions in the prisons of the Kingdom. He did not like holding people in prison for long periods that exceeded the rules for arrest and detention. But he, like many others, still considered indefinite imprisonment, even over the summer months, to be a useful tool for accelerating and forcing out a confession from a suspected criminal. He much preferred it to the use of torture, which many prosecutors still enthusiastically used.

His primary objective in the summer of 2009 was to extract the name of the man who was the likeliest suspect in the death of the Danish nurse at that ill-fated debauchery of a party. His innovations in forensic criminal investigation could no longer help him until he had this unknown man in his hands. He had to identify the red-haired man in the yellow and black checked shirt. And from the very start none of the party-goers were cooperating. Worse, he thought, they persisted in hiding the man's identity for reasons he could not comprehend. Even after a month in prison, the people he thought likeliest to know the man's identity continued to deny that they knew who he was or to recognize him from the descriptions that he had gathered from other party-goers. Were there personal reasons for this stubbornness? Or was it simply that they so strongly abhorred the idea of death by beheading which was the man's likely fate?

In talks with other prosecutors, including his deputy Ismail, he was encouraged to use more vigorous and traditional means of torture to breakdown the resolve of those who withholding the information. They all felt that the westerners especially would break down quickly and reveal just what he wanted, much sooner than their compatriots would with the application of occasional beatings or hanging from the wrists, or exposing them naked in the sun cells for a day or two (a torture the Japanese had perfected during World War Two). But Adil felt that all of these alternatives were far too likely to kill the detainees, especially the Westerners, before they could confess, and of course they would be totally ineffective in separating those who genuinely did not know the name of the suspect from those who did and could possibly confess. There was no need or justice in killing the detainees simply because they had participated in an orgy and bacchanalia, without trial or conviction. This reasoning partly explained the rationale behind Adil's scheduling for trials. He put those on trial earliest those who he believed could not help him get the murder suspect, and those for whom he had the best evidence to get a speedy trial and conviction. And of course, he had wide latitude in the types of punishment he could ask for. But for those people whom he suspected were withholding the name of the suspect, he would hold them for as long as he needed. Just the prison conditions and the heat should make them succumb before resorting to torture. He did not believe even torture would prise the name out of Adnan and at any event he had all the proof he needed to send Adnan to his public beheading. But Adil wasn't so sure about the Addisons, both Ken and Bonny. He felt certain that he could extract a confession from Khadija of her adultery without torture—that the horrible prison conditions would be enough to break her down, even before they broke her lover, who at the start of the summer was still unknown to him. The Danish girls, he thought, would cave in very soon to their horrible imprisonment conditions, but he also thought with most confidence that they did not know the name of the suspected murderer of their compatriot.

First to go to trial on his schedule was Sunithra and her lover, Mathander. Theirs was a fairly straightforward case of illicit intimacy by two unmarried people. He had what he thought was convincing proof of adultery too, but he did not want to try out that charge on the basis of the evidence he had when the lab returned a low confidence level on the reliability of the identification. To do so would ruin his chances later. Both of these Sri Lankan domestic workers confessed as well— although Adil knew that they could not possibly had understood the confession document they signed, which was written in Arabic and not translated for them. The judges returned a guilty verdict and ordered that Sunithra receive thirty lashes, and Mathander, fifty. The harshest part of their punishment was probably the immediate deportation of both of them after their lashing, without the possibility of returning to the Kingdom. This no doubt would hurt them economically. The same reasoning could be said about the deportation of Dr. Ismail

Mansu r and his wife Mishal. Adil after his interview at their house felt that they were disingenuous about not knowing that the party was a debauchery, and in saying that they did not participated. As good Muslims, they should have stayed away altogether, because it was ikhtilat, the unauthorized mixing of men and women. But instead of avoiding the party their driver revealed that they had often gone to the parties at the Addisons' house. The charges were minor, but the judge agreed that they deserved to be deported, because a good Muslim is enjoined to do good, and to avoid doing evil or what is sinful. Their sentence would also be conveyed to the other states in the Gulf Cooperative Council meaning that it was unlikely that they could get an exceptionally well-paid job—much better paid than anything he could get in the U.K. where Dr. Ismail was effectively a civil servant—in those other Arab Muslim countries. But he did not pursue either the al-Hibshi or the Zaghloul couples along those same lines. They were clearly innocent and did not know most of the other party-goers. They had made a simple mistake of accepting an invitation from Dr. Addison. They wouldn't be so imprudent again in the future. They were neither arrested nor hauled in front of the court for deportation –the al-Hibshis could not be deported in any event, because they were Saudi citizens even though they were of Yemeni descent—and they resumed their work without so much as a mild reprimand. All of these trials and punishments were carried out before the end of May.

In early June, Anna's father, Mikkel Hensen, arrived in Jeddah to reclaim the body of his daughter. He'd been informed, and invited by the Foreign Ministry, of his daughter's unfortunate death, but he did not learn that her death was probably not an accident until he arrived in the city and had an interview with Adil. When Mr. Hensen arrived at Adil's office, he had the exhausted look of someone who'd been completely wiped out by the heat. Adil invited him to sit and drink some chilled water to recover. Then he told Mr. Hensen what had happened at the party in the night and early morning leading up to Anna's fall off the balcony. Adil made it clear that he believed Anna had been murdered. He was the first to tell Mr. Hensen that they had performed an autopsy on Anna's body and discovered that she had probably had sex with her killer. Mr. Hensen was after that very upset, and he was not relieved by the offer to make a sight identification of his daughter. He declined. But then he was further upset when he learned that he would have to pay for the lead-lined coffin that would transport her body back to Denmark (The Saudis had paid for his round-trip air ticket to Jeddah.) Adil observed Mikkel Hensen closely during this brief visit. He was interested to understand if Mr. Hensen approved of his daughter's behavior. But he did not openly ask him for his reactions. He seemed indifferent when Adil told him that they did not know who killed Anna Hensdattir, but that they had a likely suspect and were searching for him. Mikkel Hensen became alarmed again when Adil asked him if he would require the death penalty for the killer, or if he could accept compensation. Mr. Hensen had no idea what compensation meant in murder cases. But he also did not approve of capital punishment, in fact, in strongly said he was against the barbaric practice of beheading. When Mr. Hensen finally left the Kingdom it was clear to Adil that his society and Mr. Hensen's did not understand or tolerate each other.

Adil decided that for his first test case of an adultery conviction using the DNA evidence as proof would best be used on the case of the young English woman, Emily, and her lover that night, the Palestinian from Jordan Subhi Muhammad. Emily had sat in her jail cell for five weeks without any visits from a lawyer or the U.K. Consul before Adil brought charges of adultery against her (and at the same time against Subhi Muhammad). She had found conditions very tough, especially the physical handling and roughing up by the "Amazon" like wardens who ran the inside of the women's prison. They would snap at her, pinch her tits through her denim uniform, or pinch her butt, or even try to goose her around the vulva. She didn't understand what they said in Arabic—they were always shouting at her whenever she emerged from her cell for meals or showers—but she gathered that they were very hostile, and would sexually assault her if she did not put up strong resistance. Early in her stay there she still had fond thoughts of the night of seduction she had enjoyed at the Addison party. Subhi had swept her away. He was so handsome, tall and strong, deeply tanned skin, and muscular arms and an obviously muscular stomach. She remembered especially the initial electricity and arousal of that party game where she had drawn Subhi as her partner. The object of the game was to move a soft red rubber ball, larger than a cricket ball, from Emily's stomach up to her neck by pressing the two partners' bodies together without using the hands on the ball. Emily had been immensely aroused right from the start as Subhi threw himself against her, rubbing his torso against hers, and pushing and pressing to raise the ball up her torso and over her breasts, finally ending with the ball tucked under his chin and locked under her chin. It had been a race, but at the time it seemed like it took forever. They won because of Subhi's intimate technique and contortions. He seemed to have caressed every square inch of her body in moving the ball up her torso—and he was so serious and earnest. All the other couples competing were constantly dropping the ball and were giggling too hard to possibly have won. As soon as he maneuvered the ball onto her neck and she held it there, he gave Emily a full open mouth kiss. It wasn't too difficult after that, and with the help of a few drinks and intimate dancing, that she knew she was going to make love to him. In fact almost every dance they had together seemed obvious to her was little more than sexual foreplay. She was ecstatic by the time he came in her—she didn't much pay attention to their undressing or to his mounting her on the couch in full view of others in the main room. She was wildly aroused by then and most of the lights were off, and most of the other party-goers had disappeared. Those memories remained vividly with her for almost a month before they began to evaporate in the hot humid climate of the prison ward, as she began to lose hope of being freed. She could not any longer hold on the memory of Subhi, his handsome face and his passionate kisses. Memory of him also faded.

Emily's parents, who lived in Jeddah and had invited her there after she had finished university, were only allowed to visit her after she had already spent a month in her baking prison. They had no news for her, although they did bring her some much-needed goods: feminine sanitary wear, some rolls of toilet paper, a bottle of vitamins, a few books, and a couple packets of sweets and six bottles of sweetened drinks—all of these things were much appreciated and she had been allowed to keep them. She also greatly appreciated the hour and a half that she spent with them in the air-conditioned interview room. Her parents were alarmed by how much weight she had apparently lost in the jail. Emily tried telling them about what she was incarcerated for, but she found it hard. She simply said that she believed she was being held for adultery. But no one had actually told her what she was in for or what her fate would be. Her parents couldn't help her understand that either. They simply did not know, and had faced a bureaucratic brick wall when they had inquired or when they had requested that she be freed.

It was in June, when daytime temperatures could rise to over 50 degrees and nighttime temperatures rarely fell below 38 degrees, that Adil came to Emily's prison to interview her. He outlined to her the next steps, namely that she was being charged with adulterous fornication, as was Subhi, and that it was a very serious crime, with very harsh sentences, including death. Adil was a little surprised when Emily seemed to brush that off without even a modicum of fear or dismay. She was above all angry with Adil and she said so, insisting that he had to release her. So he repeated the information, a threat really, that the judges could sentence her to death by stoning. "Maybe the sooner, the better for me. Any longer here in this hellhole will drive me insane." she verily shouted at him. Adil already had come to believe her when she said she had no idea about the identity of the red-headed heavyset man. She continued to maintain that she did not know who he was, nor had she noticed any such man. She continued to insist that after she fell for Subhi, she hardly noticed anyone else at the party, and besides nearly all the people there were strangers to her. Adil gave up trying to impress her with the gravity of her situation. He told her she needed to sign a confession and that things might go a little easier on her if she did. All she said, was something like, "Fuck you, raghead." Adil answered, "Well, fine. We'll see. Subhi has signed his confession, and I think you will too in a few weeks. As soon as you're ready to sign it, you can go on trial."

Three weeks later, around the end of June, Emily was taken to the showers, cleaned and given a spare haircut, and given back the clothes she had arrived in. She was numbed and not paying attention to much of anything going on around her. The extreme heat had beaten all resistance out of her. Her existence had been reduced to drinking lots of water and sweating it all off as she lay in bed hour after hour, day and night. She had even been unable to read anything that her parents had brought her. In the courtroom, where a dehumidifier and AC both ran noisily, she sat in her designated place. Her parents were not there, only some stranger who claimed he was her appointed lawyer. He seemed greasy and dark-skinned to her, with a smell of garlic. He revolted her, but at least she understood him as he spoke reasonable English. He made commentary as the trial began. The judge muttered a lot in Arabic, but Emily's eyes were glazed over and she didn't listen to her lawyer's translations. He pushed a long piece of paper with dense Arabic printing on it. "Here sign this. It's your confession of adulterous fornication on April 27th." She signed without looking at it. Then she noticed a full glass of water on the table next to her and she greedily drank it up, looking around for more. Then they had to move to another room, also cooled and waited in what looked like a corridor. When they returned, the judge walked into the room and made a short statement. Her lawyer listened intently, but she was looking around the bare room, which was adorned only with a few framed pictures that had gold lettered Arabic script on them, some words big and others smaller. "He says that the court finds you guilty, and that you are to be punished publicly by a whipping by cane, one hundred times, starting in three days. In four sessions each three days apart. And he said, "After that punishment is administered that you will be deported back to your country of origin, as will be your parents, who failed to give you the guardianship they are required to." The lawyer stood up without any further words with her and left. A bailiff led her away, back to the police van, back to the prison, back to the pale blue denim prison uniform, back to her cell and the damp mattress. The first day of caning, she screamed from the pain, but then she hardly noticed the following days, even though the caning broke through her skin in several places and caused her to bleed. It wasn't until some months later, after her slow recovery back in Essex, that she began to understand that that caning could have killed her, even before the full allotment had been meted out against her. It was some months afterwards that she was able to find out that Subhi had been beheaded around the same time as she had been caned. She could no longer remember what Subhi looked like, or that brief moment of passion that she had had with him.

It was mid-June when the French lab sent back the DNA profiles of Walter Semms, Tony Childer, and Saif Ahmad, and those results proved that Tony Childer had had sex with Khadija on the night of the party, although up to then neither of them had yet admitted that they had done so. The DNA profiles also proved that neither Walter nor Saif Ahmad had fornicated with the Danish nurse, Anna. And the skin samples taken from under Anna's nails also exonerated them. But Walter's DNA was identified as a match with what was recovered from the paper remains of the hashish joint which had been found on the balcony. Proof that he smoked hashish that night at the party. Adil would charge him with that, and he should be able to win a conviction. He decided to charge Walt right away, as the penalty of a conviction was not dire enough to force Walt to reveal the name of the unknown murder suspect, if he knew it at all. But for the other two, Tony and Saif Ahmad, Adil would have to start pressuring them. In late June he visited each of them and interviewed them in the interrogation room of the Baiji prison.

Tony Childer was an American, thirty-two years old, who had acted very self-important and self-assured when Adil had gone to the bank to arrest him. He was probably rich, but being in prison had obliterated all the little signs of wealth that he had displayed on his person. When Adil interrogated him in late June more than a month after he'd been incarcerated, Tony was a total wreck; his swagger and self-confidence were completely gone. His eyes were wild and reddened, he'd lost weight, and he'd been given a scraggly haircut. When he first entered the interrogation room, he reacted initially as if he was being hauled in from a very dark cave and he couldn't tolerate the light. On his forehead were heavy beads of sweat, and the arm pits of his tunic were stained and wet. He was directed to sit on the wooden chair at a low table opposite Adil.

"What am I doing here? Why are you holding me here? Are you charging me with something?" asked Tony in a mildly confused voice.

"In fact, Mr. Childer, we are going to take you to court for adultery. And we are going to convict you. But first we need you to sign a confession that you had adulterous sex with Khadija daughter of Abdallah on the night of 27th April. It's an important part of the trial, because we have proof of your fornication, but we need you to acknowledge that you are guilty of that."

"How can I do that? What will my wife think?"

"She'll probably be very angry with you. But that is irrelevant. I think she would have been angry with you if you had told her right away, before I arrested you. You should have thought of that before you "screwed" Khadija, to use your fine American term for having illicit sex."

"If I sign a confession can I get out of here? Can I get bail while I wait for the trial?"

"I don't think you can get bail, because of the seriousness of your crime." answered Adil. "You are on pre-trial detention, and you are a flight risk. But I understand the U.S. Consul here has applied to come visit you, you can ask him if it would be possible. He should be coming within a few weeks. Signing a confession now, will accelerate your trial, make it sooner. And I have to tell you, that Khadija signed a confession, so your refusal to sign one will only make your situation worse, and your sentence harsher."

Tony began to weep and he dropped his head onto the table.

"Mr. Childer, I need you to tell me if you knew a man at the party. He is a big man—an older man—he has red curly hair and he is heavy, even fat. He was dancing with a tall, blond Danish woman you may have noticed. Did you see such a man? Do you know who he might be? His name, do you know it?"

Tony, his head still buried in his arms on the table, shook his head as if to indicate, 'no'.

"Could you say that?" Adil asked. "Yes or no?"

Tony lifted his head and spoke slowly. "No. I didn't notice such a man. I knew hardly anyone there at that party. Khadija invited me. She works, or worked, also at the National Bank of Hijaz, with me. She was the only one I knew at the party. Except that she introduced me to her brother."

Adil continued to press, "And so you deny that you fornicated with Khadija that night?"

"No, I don't deny it. She kinda seduced me. We found a free room and one thing led to another until we were making love."

"But you didn't sleep with her through the night? Did you? Why did you leave?"

"Because I had told my wife I would be home late, but not later than four. I had to go. But she wouldn't let me take her home, because, you know, women here cannot be driven in a car with a man who is unrelated to her. And her brother wasn't going home yet when I left."

"So you'll sign a confession for me?" Adil asked.

Tony nodded in head in consent.

"Fine, I will send over a document for your signature. It will be your confession and we will submit it to the court at your trial. Maybe before the end of this month. Maybe early in July. You know of course that there is capital punishment for adulterous fornication? You may not be freed. But if you survive the lashings, you will be."

Adil left Tony Childer in the interrogation room. He was convinced that he saw a broken man; guilty of adultery, but totally and genuinely ignorant of the name of the murder suspect that Adil was seeking. On the way back to the office, Adil heard on the radio that the day's temperature had reached a record high of 51 degrees Celsius, and that it was so hot that incoming daytime flights to Jeddah International Airport were being diverted to nighttime arrivals.

After Ismail had gone to investigate into Saif Ahmad's business activities at Adnan's trading company, Adil decided to write to the Narcotics Control Police in Addis Ababa to inquire about Jameson Piper and whether this man was selling hashish. He sent off an official police inquiry letter written in English around the end of May, but he did not get a reply until the very end of July. The letter he got back was intriguing. In it the police commander for Narcotics Control wrote that they had for some time been watching this Mr. Jameson Piper because they suspected he was trading in hashish in the capital. This Mr. Piper was a Rastafarian from Shashamene in the center of the country, and they were a community well known both in Ethiopia and internationally for their growing and consumption of hashish. After they had received Colonel al-Kuthaimi's letter, they had raided Mr. Piper's office when they saw that some foreigners had gone there. They caught him in the process of dealing in hashish with these foreigners and they took him into custody. Under questioning about the invoices he had signed for transactions with Mr. Saif Ahmad al-Janbari of Jeddah, this Mr. Piper confessed that he had sold substantial volumes of hashish to this Mr. al-Janbari. But they had no evidence of Mr. al-Janbari sending or smuggling this contraband out of the country. The letter was signed by General Meklit Benhare, head of the Narcotics Control Division in Addis Ababa for the National Police.

Adil finished reading the letter and let out a small cheer. "I've got him now." He went and told Ismail of the additional information they had gotten from Ethiopia and that they would take Saif to court on charges of narcotics smuggling with proof. While he was telling Ismail this news, Samir, the head of the forensics lab, came into Ismail's office and he listened to what Adil was telling Ismail. Samir then stepped in. "You know, you might remember, we collected some small samples of the cannabis that was smoked that night at the party. It's enough to be able to examine it and see where it came from. We can try to match its genetic code to that of cannabis that is grown in this place in Ethiopia. If they match then it would prove that what Saif Ahmad smoked that night came from Ethiopia and was probably what he himself bought there and smuggled into the Kingdom."

Adil had not thought of this, but of course this was just the sort of forensic investigations he had wanted when he first introduced forensics and set up the laboratory. "You'll have to get the cooperation of the Ethiopian criminal forensics lab. Maybe they already have a genetic signature for their local grown cannabis so that they can spot imported material." Adil had no idea how long this process might take, but he expected it could run to several months. But he would probably take Saif Ahmad to court even without the results of matching cannabis.

In mid-June, Bonny Addinson was brought before the court on charges of procuring young women for an orgy. The entire procedure took less than twenty minutes from the time that she stepped into the courtroom to the time when the judge stood up and made to leave. The trial was entirely in Arabic and no one was on hand to translate for Bonny. She was not asked any questions. And she was uncertain what had happened during the short hearing. At the end of the hearing a slight man dressed in the national costume of white dishdasha and white keffiya approached her from the side and said to her in clear English:

"The judge finds you guilty of procuring women for indecent purposes, and for spreading vice. And he has sentenced to you to a punishment of twenty lashes by the cane, to be administered as soon as possible, and then to be promptly expulsed from the Kingdom."

Bonny looked a little confused. "Excuse me, but who are you?"

"I am your court appointed lawyer."

"But you didn't say anything during the whole trial."

The young lawyer shrugged his shoulders and said, "There was no need. Nothing for me to say. No defense for you, really. Procedurally everything was correct."

Bonny felt a little relieved that her ordeal was nearing completion and that soon she would have her freedom restored and she would be leaving the Kingdom forever. But she underestimated how much twenty lashes hurt and they came as a shock to her from the very first time the cane landed on her back. She had been lain on the ground supinely, dressed in normal street clothes, when the flogging started. The lashings of the cane were not gentle, and this punishment was not primarily about shaming the victim. When she finally arrived back in

England and could undress and look at her backside, she still had six or seven clear blue-black bruises that ran across her and middle lower back and her buttocks, clearly outlining the shape of an elongated cane. Her hatred for all things Saudi grew even more. "Swine." She hissed to herself while standing at the mirror. Flogging had to be the most primitive and barbaric of punishments, she thought to herself.

Unknown to Bonny at the same time she had her trial, her lover Walt— who on the night of the party had claimed to her that he couldn't make love to her because the marijuana made it difficult to have an erection—was being tried for smoking a narcotic drug, namely hashish, a vice which was considered to be very serious. He had spent about a fortnight less in prison, but had equally been left in the dark that whole period. Adil was very proud that he was able to bring evidence of Walt's smoking through the investigations of his forensics laboratory, which matched DNA found the remnants of a joint paper to Walt's sample of DNA material. Walt had signed a confession as well, which he didn't think meant much and which he could not understand whether it would lighten or make worse his punishment. As he expected he was found guilty and but was not expected was that his sentence was to receive fifty lashes and to be expelled from the Kingdom.

Back in his home country in Wales, Walt did not know if he should try and contact Bonny. But to contact her would require first a complicated search for her, and he did not know where to start. First of all, he did not know Bonny's maiden name or where she originally came from, nor her last home address with Ken before she had moved to Jeddah with him. By the end of the summer, Walter had begun to completely forget about Bonny. It had been a strange affair with her, pushed forward mainly by Bonny's anger at Ken's serial philandering, and Walt's boredom, and it had ended at a very strange, unsatisfactory party evening. He felt he had been harshly punished for what he had considered to have been at best a misdemeanor. In the months after his return home, he did not for a moment realize that had he not smoked that joint with guys he didn't really know or like he probably would have made love to Bonny that night in the wee hours after the party, and probably he would not have gone home early so that he would have in all likelihood been arrested and charged with adultery, the outcome of which would have been much more serious for him. He did not like to think about his last months in Jeddah. He did however thank God that he was back in a lovely mild climate where he enjoyed his freedom walking outdoors. He joined a local choir and began to build a new life, writing off his entire four years' experience in Jeddah as a complete and total loss, best forgotten.

In early July Adil next took to trial the two Danish nurses that he had found, nearly completely naked and in tight embrace sleeping together, Lisbeth and Vigga. He charged them with engaging in homosexual activities, which actually was not in the Sharia, but which was very sternly treated by Saudi tradition. They were tried separately on different days but they both took very nonchalant views about their situation, and they were quick to sign confessions. Adil was not surprised when a guilty verdict was handed down, but he was surprised at the harshness of the punishment. They each would get 50 lashes of the cane on a public square at the same time. The canings were to be given over three sessions, each spaced three days apart. After receiving that flogging, they were to be deported, and banned from ever returning to the Kingdom. When the sentence was translated for them, they each in their own turn rather shrugged it off, and when they got the lashing, they were stoical. They were very glad to be leaving Saudi Arabia; they mostly worried that their other two colleagues, Elsa and Agnate, might get the death penalty by stoning. People in the prison told them that no one survived the stoning. Once they were told that their sentences were limited to only 50 lashes of the cane, they both resolved to bear it and hold their breath until they could be sent home.

Also in early July, Adil received the signed confession back from Tony. He was ready to go to court for his trial. He had no expectations that he might receive the harshest of capital punishments. The judge at first was reluctant to accept the proof based on the recovered semen and the identification by matched DNA profiles. He still wanted the four witnesses of the act of fornication, but of course there were no such witnesses. Adil protested that a man's semen found in the woman's vagina was better proof of fornication than the word of four different witnesses who think they saw a couple in the very act of penetrative sex, which may or may not have resulted in the man ejaculating into the woman. The judge had a hard time believing that a man seen copulating with a woman, would not have already ejaculated his semen. But Adil scorned this idea. He pointed out that not all men ejaculate with every coupling, and then most men only ejaculate at their climax, which could take several minutes of "priming the pump" and receiving maximum arousal from the woman. So there were undoubtedly many couplings where the man did not inseminate the woman. And so merely witnessing what appeared to be fornication, was not proof of insemination and thus adultery. Only recovering fresh semen from the woman was definitive proof, and the reason that that had not been accepted as proof in the original days when the doctors of jurisprudence were arguing the evidences needed to prove adultery as based on the sunnah ("the right practices and sayings") of Muhammad was simply that in Muhammad's days there was not the scientific knowledge about insemination and the means of identifying semen. The determination of adultery from the beginnings of Islamic law was a less precise and well-defined concept than what people in the present day were able to specify. The judge was still uncomfortable with the arguments that Adil put forward and especially with the frank and open discussion about sexual anatomy and the sexual act, but he realized eventually that his discomfort came out of his prudishness and his total unfamiliarity of the technical terms. After all the evidence of the prosecutor was presented—which included the photographs of a naked Khadija in the bed and then standing next to the bed on the morning of the 27 of April, photos which the judge cast a prurient eye over for some minutes—the judge asked if he could excuse himself to consult with one of the doctors of law on these very issues that Adil had introduced. He asked for the trial to reconvene the next morning. Tony was overwhelmed. He thought that he had been condemned to death by beheading. And he collapsed to the floor bawling as soon as he tried to stand up.

The next day was another scorcher with the temperature rising to 50 degrees by noon. The court room was cooler than outside of course but it was stuffy and about 34 degrees. The judge returned and after he sat down, he reviewed what had been presented the day before. Then he outlined the guidance he had received during the recess. Then he issued his reasoning about how he arrived at a guilty verdict, and especially decisive he said in this case, was the confession that the court had received from Anthony Childer and the corroborating confession they had received from Khadija daughter of Abdullah. In passing the guilty verdict in this case, the defendant was deserving of the penalty fitting the seriousness of this crime. So he pronounced a sentence of 1000 lashes to be administered in equal portions over forty days with a day in between each flogging, in other words 50 lashes of the cane every other day over 40 days. Again when this was translated for Tony Childer, he collapsed crying and wailing that he would not survive, he would not survive. His defense lawyer said that he would appeal the verdict and the punishment.

The appeal did not change the verdict, but the punishment was reduced to 500 lashes distributed over twenty days. Adil was not at all certain that Tony in his broken-down state could survive even 500 lashes. And in fact in early August after receiving 350 lashes, Tony expired in the midst of the next flogging session. It was a month later that the foreign press learned about the death by flogging of an American citizen for adultery and they made a big fuss trying to shame Washington into a formal protest. The British government issued a limp denunciation of the use of capital punishment for minor crimes. But like all late summer news, the story faded into oblivion long before September, and the American and British governments did not have to put any diplomatic pressure on the Saudi regime.

In that interim between Tony Childer's execution and the end of summer—actually Ramadan which started at the end of August—Adil saw the opportunity to continue pushing for adultery convictions based on DNA profiling. And the easiest to bring to trial were the remaining two Danish nurses, Elsa and Agnate. He brought Agnate to trial in late July. It was a straightforward trial for adulterous fornication, because they had the photo and video evidence of Adnan copulating on top of her and they had the witness statements of Adil, and the other three police agents who entered the room with him. Furthermore, they had Agnate's confession statement. And in addition, Adil was counting on the continuing animus and insult that informed Saudis felt towards all things Danish—so much so that he didn't need to raise that issue, it popped out in one of the comments of the presiding judge, something along the lines, "And of course those godless Danish people who mock and pour bile and urinate on our Holy Book and our Prophet…" The trial went quickly and the conviction was almost a certainty beforehand. But the judge did not mandate death by stoning—he could have and that would have added to the shock of the news—but instead he required that Agnate receive 200 lashes of the cane in public spread over twenty days, that is twenty lashes every other day, followed by expulsion. Before Ramadan started Agnate was already back in her original home in Copenhagen, smarting and bearing awful welts, but recovering well and trying to push Jeddah out of her mind.

It was already clear that Adil was not one of those affluent Jeddah residents who could afford to leave the city during the height of the summer heat. After his wife had their two children over the previous three years, he could no longer afford the long foreign break to escape the heat. This motivated him to clean up all the cases of the party-goers before Ramadan. He still felt his highest priority was to find and convict the killer of Anna, but he had not advanced that investigation very much at all since the end of May.

About the beginning of August, it was Elsa's turn to go to court on adultery charges. Adil's case was not as ironclad as it had been for Agnate, because they did not have the additional evidence of witnesses of the fornication with Ken. But Adil had the good fortune of getting the same judge who had presided over Tony Childer's case, and he had already been converted to the precedent of accepting DNA profiling of a man's semen found in a woman's vagina as definitive proof. This judge also was biased against the Danish woman for the reason of the Muhammad cartoon scandal—judges gossip amongst themselves about such things. He brought in a conviction, but only imposed a punishment of 100 lashes of the cane administered over ten days. And Elsa was deported before the middle of August. Adil felt pleased he had remaining in prison only four detainees out of the twenty or so original party-goers he had arrested, and all four of them could probably give him the name, and maybe even the whereabouts, of the probable killer of Anna, but for reasons he still could not make out, they refused to tell him. His murder case was still far from being solved. And now he felt that it was time to start imposing some real pressure on the three men to get some answers. He now felt certain that Khadija did not know the identity of his prime suspect.

And that meant that Adil needed to tell those three men, Dr. Ken Addison, Adnan bin Abdullah al-Misha'ri, and Saif Ahmad al-Janbari, that he was going to turn the tourniquet tighter if they did not cooperate with him, and that their punishments for the charges they would face would be much harsher than perhaps they already thought. Dr. Ken and Adnan already faced the very real possibility of being beheaded, but it was Saif Ahmad against whom Adil could bring the greatest pressure, because he did not at the beginning of August have the evidence and proof of narcotics smuggling against him that could possibly lead to his execution by beheading. He was still waiting at that point to get further evidence from Ethiopia. So Adil resolved that after a talking to and a stern warning that if Saif still refused to tell him the name of the heavyset red-headed man he would be hung up by his wrists in the full glare of the sun until he confessed. Saif, as Adil expected, refused to say anything and refused to confess his crimes of narcotics and alcohol smuggling even after threatened. But Adil was very surprised when the warden called him after having "hung him out to dry" for only part of one day, Saif caved in and wanted to confess and tell him all. He wasn't as hard-bitten as he made out to be.

Saif had been hosed down as they took him down after four hours in the direct sun. Then they gave him ample amounts of chilled water and returned him to his cells where there was a clean prison uniform waiting for him. Adil came later that evening after Saif had eaten a light meal of porridge and fruit.

"And now, Saif son of Ahmad, you have to tell me, you know the name of the tall, heavyset, foreigner who was at the same party with you and wearing a yellow and black-checked short sleeve shirt, don't you?"

Saif nodded.

"And the reason you would not tell me his name is that he was an important member of your smuggling ring for wine and spirits, isn't that right?"

"Yes, that is right. And because he is a friend of the Shaykh, our employer and the man who directs our smuggling."

"So tell me, what is his name?"

"He Matthew Enders. Captain Matthew Enders. He is Scottish and he works for the Bank."

"Which bank is that, specifically?"

"The Shaykh's Bank, the National Bank of the Hijaz."

"And you saw him at the party and you recognized and acknowledged him there?"

"Yes, he was at the party."

"And he was dancing and acting amorously with the blond Danish nurse whom he later killed?"

"Yes, he was. But I don't know and I didn't see him kill anyone?"

"You didn't see him fornicate with her and then throw her off the balcony?"

"No, neither the former nor the latter. I saw them dancing with her. His hands were all over her body and he had a hard-on like you wouldn't believe, seemed to break out of his trousers. I remember seeing that and that impressed me at the time. But then I left the party."

"When?"

"Oh I don't know, about two o'clock I guess."

"You came with Adnan to the party. But you left without him. So did you walk home?"

"No I took a taxi."

"Then how did you know to flee home?"

"Captain Matt's driver called me later that morning, saying that he had fled the party and then left the country by the boat."

"So you know about the boat?"

"Of course."

"You'll confess to smuggling in the wine and spirits through Captain Matt's yacht?"

"Yes."

"And you'll confess to smuggling in hashish bought in Addis Ababa from a Mr. Piper?"

"How did you know that?"

"Detective work. It's my job."

"We've even identified the hashish that you smoked that night at the party—because you didn't burn it all up—with the sort of hashish that you regularly bought from Mr. Piper." Adil knew he was telling a little lie. He still hadn't received any word back from the Ethiopians about the genetic make-up of the local cannabis and the scraps of unsmoked cannabis they had found in Adnan's car and on the balcony. But he expected that they would get those results sometime soon.

Saif said, "Oh. I didn't know you could do that."

"So will you sign a confession that you also smuggled narcotics into the Kingdom? We would need you to tell us how you carried the hashish you bought in your luggage and into the country."

"It's a death sentence for me, isn't it?"

"Most probably. They beheaded a pair of Pakistanis in the Eastern Province three months ago for smuggling in punk through their luggage. And by the way, tell me how did you and Captain Matt get the alcohol past the customs officers at the port?"

"The Shaykh paid the chief customs officer there a bribe in advance of each delivery to overlook the unmarked cartons we unloaded. They all turned the other way when we picked up the goods and carried them away. Only at night, of course."

"And the goods were not kept at your trading company office."

"Of course not. We hired another warehouse outside the port area."

"Fine. I promise that you will not be hung up in the sun again. But I cannot promise you any leniency, because I have no sway over the decisions of the judges."

"Sure, I understand."

"I will bring you to trial as soon as possible. Probably before Ramadan."

"And what about Adnan? What about him?"

"Well he is facing the death penalty for adulterous fornication. Looks almost certain that he will be beheaded. Why do you ask?"

"He's my friend, and a good mate."

"Tell me do you know where this Captain Matt probably is hiding over the past three months?"

"I don't. But I know he keeps an apartment in Cyprus. And that he buys his goods that he imports there."

"Fine thank you. If he's there, we will probably find his yacht there. The Chrysanthemum. That's its name, isn't it?"

"Yes, I seem to remember it was a flower."

As Adil was leaving the interrogation room in the prison he was feeling as if his entire case—the foreigners' party—was opening up for him and that everything was going to be solved. He would get his hands on Captain Matthew Enders and that would provide the proof of his adultery with and murder of poor innocent Anna. He felt his time spent in Jeddah this summer had been well spent, and successful. He would try to get more information from Saif Ahmad about Shaykh Abdullah's smuggling activities in order to bring charges against the great man. But he thought he could still take Saif Ahmad to trial before Ramadan. And that left the question of when to take Khadija to trial, whether before or after Ramadan. He no longer needed to press her to get Captain Matt's name; he already had it. She only faced adultery charges and he could now, after Tony's sentence, probably extract a confession from her. The only question that he thought remained for Khadija was whether she would be sentenced to death by stoning—a harsh sentence and a truly awful punishment—or if she would receive a lesser, meaning non-fatal, sentence of lashes which she could possibly survive. He would bring the final adultery cases against Adnan and Dr. Ken in early October after Ramadan and the Eid celebrations were over.

In the final week before the start of Ramadan that year, which would likely be on the 31st of August, Adil still had not gotten an answer from the Ethiopians about the matching of the genetic make-up of the hashish that had been in Saif's possession and the hashish that Mr. Piper usually sold. Adil believed he had a strong enough case to take Saif to court without the additional corroborating information from the Ethiopian Narcotics Police. He got a date for Saif's trial on the 26th on charges of participating in a smuggling ring importing wine, spirits, and hashish. The trial was longer than all the others he had prosecuted that summer and it wasn't until the next day that all the evidence was presented and the judge began to consider the verdict. As Adil expected the judge brought in a verdict of guilty, but unexpectedly he sentenced Saif Ahmad to death by beheading, the harshest penalty he could apply. Before adjourning the court, the judge said that the punishment would not be imposed until the first Friday after the end of Eid. Fridays were the customary day for public executions.

As the high summer ran into Ramadan, all that was left on Adil's calendar was getting Captain Matt back into the Kingdom.

Illegal migrant workers

Shortly before Ramadan, Adil got an unexpected call from a sergeant from the immigration police. They had found Muhammad, Captain Matthew's Eritrean driver. He was living in a poor district of the city near the industrial port in a hovel that was housing more than a dozen illegal Eritrean workers. They had arrested him and then discovered that Adil's department was looking for him. Adil was pleased to hear the news and he asked the policeman to bring him to his offices. He was not to be deported before Adil had the chance to interview him.

About two hours later a shurta officer brought Muhammad to Adil's office. He saluted Adil and left. Muhammad was a light chocolate colored black man from Eritrea, slim and short, dressed in dirty rags and flip-flops., with a stubble of a ruddy beard on his chin. He smiled embarrassed at Adil unaware that he had done anything wrong.

Adil asked him for his name. The little man broke into a big smile. "Muhammad Mansur al-Habashi" in accented Arabic.

"Do you know how to speak Arabic?"

Muhammad answered in a typical local Arabic expression "shouwai, shouwai" which was used often to mean 'just a little bit'. He used his hands to show a small amount.

Adil continued speaking to him in Arabic, slowly and clearly enunciating his words.

"When was the last time you saw Captain Matthew Enders?"

"You mean, Captain Matt, the afranji? I never knew his family name."

"Yes. That one. The Dutchman. Or the Scotsman."

"The last time I saw him was when I dropped him at the pier at his big boat, in the marina port. That was already a long time ago. Maybe May, maybe the end of April. I then went back to his house. I waited there for a few days, but he never returned. On the fourth day, I left and went to my co-nationals' house. I've been there ever since."

"When did Captain Matt go to his boat? Do you remember the time?"

"Oh yes, it was just at the time when the mu'ezzin began calling for Dawn prayer. Still dark. I remember that well. The loudspeaker was very loud and seemed like it was right over our heads when we arrived. He was all night at the party."

"And where was that party?"

"At the doctor's house in Lutfiya Street."

"You had been there before? You knew the doctor?"

"Oh, no sir. I mean. I don't know the doctor and I've never seen him. But I took Captain Matt to that house in Lutfiya Lane many times over the past few years."

"And how did you know it was a party?"

"He told me, and he told me to wait for him. He said all night, if necessary. He's a good man, that Captain. He gave me two, one hundred riyal notes when he left the car, before he ran down the pier to his boat. Is he in some trouble?"

"Yes."

"Am I in some trouble too?"

"Well, you are working illegally here in the Kingdom and don't have a registered passport showing when you entered, and whether you entered properly. But other than that, no, you are not in trouble. You will be deported."

Muhammad smiled sheepishly at Adil and then looked down at his feet and shifted his weight from one leg to the other and back again. Adil continued.

"You were his regular driver?"

"Yes. I drove him to his work in the morning and in the afternoon drove him to wherever he needed to go. And then back home. Every day."

"Where was his work?"

"At the bank, of course."

"When you drove Captain Matt to the party was anyone else in the car with him?"

"No."

"And when he left from the doctor's house, did anyone leave with him?"

"No. He was the only one to leave at that time. He was still putting on his shirt in the car. He was in a big hurry."

"And you drove him straight to his ship? You didn't pass by his house?"

"Yes, just as he told me to."

"You spent part of the night talking with your countryman, Abdal Aziz an-Nasiri?"

"Oh yes. He's a good man. But he had to leave when his masters left the party some few hours earlier. Is he in trouble?"

"Actually yes. He's now unemployed after we deported his masters; Dr and Mrs Ismail Mansur were deported. But that's not important. Did you see or hear anything strange around the ground floor of the house between the time Abdal Aziz left and Captain Matt came out in a hurry, half dressed?"

"No, nothing."

"But you were parked in the ground floor open parking area under the house so if there were a disturbance at the front of the house on the street you would have heard it, no?"

"Maybe. But I was parked in the back of the house away from the street by the little back alley."

"Tell me the truth, so help you God. You heard and saw nothing. Were you inside your car?"

"Actually, after Abdal Aziz drove his masters away, I got back in the car. And I must admit, by God's word, that I probably fell asleep. It was very late, you see. I did nothing wrong. I didn't hear or see anything, as best I can remember, until Captain Matt got into the car."

Now Muhammad was twitching much more, and his grin had disappeared. He had a worried look on his face.

"Was there something wrong that I should have noticed out on the street that night?" Muhammad asked timidly.

"Possibly. And Captain Matt, once he was back in the car, he didn't tell you anything about why he was going to his ship? He didn't tell you that he was planning on sailing away?"

"No. But he never shared with me what he was thinking or planning on doing. He did tell me once we got there—I mean to the pier—to go back to the house and not to wait for him."

"So why did you wait two or three days for him at his house, as you just told me?"

"There was no place else for me to go. I needed to stand by the car, to protect it and to be ready to take the Captain to wherever he needed to be taken."

Adil indicated that that was enough. He called for the serjeant and told him to take Muhammad back to the migrant detention center and do with him whatever they needed to do. He had no further need for Muhammad.

"Thank you, sir. Thank you. I hope I was of help to you."

"Go in peace," said Adil as he waved off the Eritrean who was momentarily relieved that he wasn't going to face some stern punishment or a beating.

Adil wrote down all the notes of his interview. He was not pleased. They had already confirmed Captain Matthew's identity, that he was at the party and that he had been close dancing with Anna. No, still no one had witnessed Anna's fall or impact. Still she could have fallen accidentally off the balcony after Captain Matthew left in a hurry. She could have passed out in a blind drunk and fallen over the railing as she was looking over to wave goodbye to him. She could have jumped in a deliberate act. Suicide. Heartbroken suicide. Or it could have been that the Captain made love to her and pushed her off the balcony over the railing—either deliberately or accidentally. And there was still the possibility, although remote, that someone else may have pushed her over after the Captain left. A man jealous and wanting to have sex with her when he found her passed out on the sofa nearly naked and voluptuous and just ready to be had again. But such a man was still unidentified. Murder, accident, suicide, or some act unrelated to Captain Matthew—none of these possibilities could be ruled out. The only thing for certain that Adil had was that the DNA from the semen samples on and in Anna's body as well as the DNA of the material taken from under her nails did not match the DNA of any of the other men that they had identified who were probably at that party up to the moment of Anna's plunge. They would have to take Captain Matthew into custody to test his DNA to see if he was the man responsible for the DNA left on Anna's body. But that still left him with no proof. He needed motivation. A confession would help and it seemed that only Captain Matthew had been in a position to be able to give them a confession. But they did not have Captain Matt. He was out of the country, and out of reach. All this put Adil into a vile mood. He left his office shortly afterwards for Maghrib prayer as it was nearly sunset and the mu'ezzin would be shouting out at any moment.

A deal to snare a Shaykh

It was late August, but before the start of Ramadan when Adil got the phone call from the Deputy Minister's office. It was a call that he had to pay the utmost respect to. When the Deputy Minister of the Interior for the entire Hijaz, His Excellency Prince Abdul Aziz al-Turki al-Saudi—both your ultimate boss and the most powerful man in the entire western part of the country—calls requesting your attendance, you have to pay close attention and be most self-abasing. Adil had only met and been in Prince Abdel Aziz's presence twice before. Those times, he had shaken the Prince's limp hand, bowed his head to the Prince, muttered the ritual salutations, and taken his place in the second rank of attendees. Those times were in the Prince's personal divan. This time, the Prince's office required that Adil come at eleven o'clock to the Prince's public divan in the Ministry building, dressed in his normal national costume, and not in his khaki investigator's uniform. This meant Adil would be attending both as a representative of one of second most important tribes from the southern region of Najran—the Al Kuthaimi—as well as a representative of the office of the Prosecutor and Investigator for Jeddah, a branch of the Ministry of Interior.

Adil arrived promptly at eleven o'clock at the receptionist desk in the Ministry the next morning. He was dressed in a crisply pressed white dishdasha, and on his head he wore a red and white checked keffiya with a black head cord, and as well he sported a gold Swiss watch, and on his feet he wore a pair of light-weight Italian designer slip-on shoes—his best, most expensive clothes. He was led up an escalator to a second-floor room—the small public divan—and he was asked to have a seat on a low red couch which lined the western wall about eight feet from a raised dais and cushioned seat on the southern wall. That latter was where the Prince would no doubt sit. Adil was the only one there. A bare headed black man dressed in a caftan with a black embroidered vest came over to him and offered to bring him either tea or coffee. This was going to be a formal meeting, thought Adil, but he was still at a loss about what the subject could be for this meeting. He would not be taking notes at a meeting such as this meeting. He'd have to listen carefully for nuances as well as direct statements by the Prince.

The servant came back and poured him a small cup of coffee from a very large parrot-beaked silver coffee pot. As he set the cup down on a small low table in front of Adil, another man was shown in the room. Adil knew at once who this tall slender man was. He stood up for him. He was as-Sayyid Abdul Hamid bin Muhammad al-Kindi, a mufti and a senior member of the Council of senior scholars, in other words a jurisprudent who oversaw the work and legal reasoning and decisions of judges for the entire Kingdom, a kind of supreme judge and administrator combined, who usually sat in the capital. Abdul Hamid came over to Adil and shook his hand and greeted him warmly and sincerely with a nice smile. It had been a very long time since they had last met and talked, but Abdul Hamid seemed to have remembered Adil well. Then he took a seat on the red couch just opposite Adil and gave his drinks order to the servant.

They were seated only about six feet apart across the narrow divan room.

After asking after Adil's family, how many children he had—he had two young children—and how his parents were faring, Abdul Hamid stated:

"I hear that you are introducing a lot of new technologies to evidence gathering in your office. And you are introducing this new evidence into your prosecutions. You have to be praised for your innovative approach to your job. You have definitively shaken up a lot of conservative literalist judges down here."

"Thank you, Sidi. I try to serve the objective of the law and not merely introduce innovation for its own sake, as we were taught in our jurisprudence courses on the implementation of the Sharia. We were taught to apply mental effort and not merely conformity."

"You were taught correctly, my son. It is only a shame that so many of our judges can only conform and imitate past practices without any independent thinking or mental effort. You have made their work more difficult for certain. They have to think hard. I can only say, carry on with what you're doing."

The as-Sayyid took up his glass of tea and sipped slowly.

"I suppose you know already, but we have earlier this summer asked a number of our best jurisprudential senior scholars to examine and rule on the new evidence you have introduced as proof of adultery. They have taken all your arguments to mind and will issue a fatwa soon."

"That would be good, God willing." said Adil who could not detect whether from the Sayyid's voice he supported or was against Adil's use of semen marking to prove adultery or rape.

They again fell silent.

After another ten minutes the doors to the divan opened and in came Prince Abdul Aziz al-Turki dressed in his uniform of a white dishdasha underneath a black, gold bordered sheer light cloak, and wearing his white keffiya with a thick black head band holding it place. He was escorted by two assistants and two bodyguards. One assistant went straight to a cushioned seat next to the Prince's raised seat. The Prince silently entered the room and went first to as-Sayyid Abdul Hamid and lightly embraced him by the shoulders and gave him a formal kiss on both cheeks. The Sayyid said, "Your Excellency, I am honored to see you again." The Prince said something softly that Adil could not hear. Then he came over to Adil and offered his hand to him and shook it lamely. He smiled but did not meet Adil's eyes. Adil himself bowed his head and then took the hand he shook the Prince's with and touched his forehead with it, a sign of respect and lower rank. Then the Prince went and sat down in his seat of cushions. The bodyguards remained standing next to him on both sides blocked the view of the assistants who were seated behind them.

"I want to thank both of you for coming on such short notice to talk with me. And especially you, as-Sayyid Abdul Hamid. Coming all the way from Riyadh. I suppose you might be curious about the business I want to consult with you about." The Prince smiled as he spoke but did not look directly at either of the two men.

"Colonel Adil, I want especially to commend you for the fine investigative work you have been doing in recent months, both against enemies of the state who plot to overthrow the Al Saud, but also your investigation into that debauchery and murder which occurred a few months ago in a foreigner's house. I want to encourage you in your efforts to enforce the Sharia in this country and I hope you continue."

"But in your investigations, you have uncovered two adulterers from the same family, a family of a very important and powerful man here in the city. A certain shaykh and tribal leader of a cadet branch of our family, who runs many important businesses in the city. He is a man who has accrued too much power and behaves as if he were above the law which he violates with impunity. We presume you know who I mean."

Adil of course knew exactly that he meant Adnan and Khadija's father, Shaykh Abdullah bin Amr al-Misha'ri, who was the chairman of the National Bank of the Hijaz and Deputy Mayor of Jeddah.

"He has too much power, which he uses without regards to our prerogatives. He violates the Sharia prohibition on interest on debt.

His bank charges interest and pays usurious interest payments on investments to its clients. This has increasingly distressed us and as well others in our family. And we need to suppress this behavior."

"I have now for several months had my secret intelligence agents looking into his affairs. And it seems they have found evidence which suggests that this Shaykh is behind a ring of contraband importers. That this ring which my men believe is run by the Shaykh's son on his behalf, imports illegal alcohol and spirits and sells the same around the city. But it hard to find proof of this. We cannot find how it is or through what agency that the Shaykh or his son imports the alcohol into Jeddah. And we also believe that they import narcotics into the Kingdom, but likewise have not uncovered the means by which they do this." The Prince paused and looked in the direction of Adil as if seeking a response from him.

After a respectful silence of a few minutes, Adil spoke up: "If I may, Your Excellency, our investigation of the debauchery you mentioned which occurred in late April, did uncover evidence and testimony that the Shaykh's son, Adnan, brought cases of illegal wine and whiskey to that party. But we too have not discovered how he obtained these cases. They were unmarked cartons, so clearly they were smuggled into the country."

"And do you have any ideas about the means through which this contraband is smuggled in?" said the Prince who was looking at the Sayyid.

"Our suspicions point, as you rightly surmised, to Bank. And we think that a large yacht which is apparently owned by the Bank is used to smuggle in the contraband, both alcohol and narcotics. And that the contraband is then taken to a warehouse of a trading company owned by this Adnan."

"And my sources tell me that you're currently holding Adnan under arrest for adultery. And his sister too for fornication with another unrelated man. Is this right?" said the Prince.

"Yes, that is right."

The Prince continued: "And with the innovative evidence you now collect you can bring charges against both of them that require capital punishment. Am I right? Very serious charges, very extreme punishments. Public beheading and public stoning as required for these very serious crimes. Not to mention heavy penalties for smuggling and selling contraband alcohol. Penalties so heavy and terrible, and of course shameful, that a certain powerful, rich man might seek to subvert the course of justice by a certain contribution of monies to one or two or more judges who could rule on these cases? Especially if their conviction hinged on your new innovative evidence to prove guilt?" The Prince looked at as-Sayyid. Adil concluded at once from that glance that the Shaykh had already tried to bribe one or more judges who would hear Adnan's case and that as-Sayyid being a noble, just man, told the Prince of this attempt.

Adil broke the silence. "Our office is also investigating a case of murder or a killing which occurred at this debauchery. We don't have proof yet, but it seems that the killer has absconded with a large yacht and is abroad apparently. This man, who we believe is the prime suspect in the murder, may also be the smuggler. But we can't prove this yet. But all testimony so far points at this. We still need to conduct a DNA profile on this man to confirm that he was at the party, that he adulterously used one of the foreign women there, and then dumped her off the balcony, killing her. And then he fled the country in this boat, owned supposedly by the Bank."

"Well, well, well." said the Prince. "You are a very clever, very thorough investigator, Adil son of Ahmad. So you know this man's name? And his current whereabouts?"

"Yes, we do know his name, and we believe he is located somewhere in the Mediterranean. Probably Cyprus."

"Then we need to lure him back with a cargo of contraband to prove the connection between him and the Shaykh's smuggling business." said the Prince.

"But we don't have enough evidence to be able to extradite this Scotsman."

"I'm not talking about extradition, Adil son of Ahmad. We have no extradition agreements with EU countries. You are going to bring Adnan to trial on charges of adulterous fornication, am I right? And the judges will find him guilty, using your innovative evidence and proof, and they can sentence him to the utmost of punishments as prescribed by Sharia. Am I right, as-Sayyid?"

"Yes, if Adil son of Ahmad has the proof as required by our jurisprudence, the judges can apply the most serious of punishments." as-Sayyid said calmly.

"But sir, I do not have to use my innovative evidence. We meet the traditional proof of four living witnesses who caught Adnan in the blaze of adultery." Adil was trying to translate 'in flagrante delicto' into Arabic. "I have four witnesses, including myself, who will swear an oath that he committed penetrative sex with a woman who is not his wife. And we have both photos and videos as well."

"So Abdul Hamid, does this take away from our judges all latitude in making a ruling on the punishment?"

"No, Your Excellency. They can still apply their judgment in the case and have some liberty to apply either beheading or lashing unto death, or even a lashing that the sinner may survive."

"So I thought." said the Prince almost gleefully. "And for the Shaykh's daughter? Do you also have definitive proof of her adultery, or must you rely on this DNA evidence?"

"No, for Khadija daughter of Abdullah, I have only the evidence of DNA taken from semen found inside her woman's secret organ."

"And our judges in this fair, just city, may decide to reject that evidence as proof and may even acquit her. Isn't that right, as-Sayyid?"

"Yes, Your Excellency. You know well the law and its conduct."

"Yes. We don't want a public stoning of a noble unwed woman in this city. We will all be shamed," the Prince continued.

"Fine. Now my fine friends, we will wait here for the Shaykh to come to us here and then we will talk with him to see how he might propose to save his children from destruction and public shame and disgrace. I expect he's already waiting for us downstairs."

After ten minutes when they were again served tea or coffee and small dishes of date and nut confectionary, the doors to the divan were again opened and in came a small man dressed in a white thaub (a slightly different cut and form than the dishdasha) and a red and white checked keffiya, and also Italian slip on shoes. He had, unusual for a Hijazi tribesmen, very light skin, almost ashen in color, perhaps from his age. Adil had never met Shaykh Abdullah bin Muhammad al-Misha'ri in person before but he noticed that his son Adnan bore little resemblance to him. The Shaykh smiled a small modest smile and went directly over to the Prince, who had stood up, and they embraced and kissed on the cheeks. But they scarcely said anything one to the other. Adil did hear the Shaykh whisper something like, "Your Excellency". It was a very brief and unfriendly greeting. The minimum required. The Prince then directed the Shaykh to his right and introduced him to as-Sayyid Abdul Hamid bin Muhammad al-Kindi who shook hands with the Shaykh mummering some formulaic greetings. And then to his left the Prince introduced him to Colonel Adil bin Ahmad al-Kuthaimi from the Jeddah office of the Chief Prosecutor and Investigator. (It was a subtle signal from the Prince of what the Shaykh might expect from this meeting.) The Shaykh crossed the room and looking Adil deep in the face, with a weak smile, he shook his hand firmly. Adil again showed his lower rank by bowing his head a little, and bringing his hand up to his forehead after he had shaken the Shaykh's. "Now if you please, my dear Shaykh," said the Prince, "I insist that you come sit here next to me." The Prince pointed to a spot between him and the Sayyid, the most favored of all seats in the divan, on the right hand and closest to the Prince.

"I am so glad that you were able to come today, my dear friend." said the Prince with a faint insincere smile. "Especially on such short notice."

"Your wish is my command," said the Shaykh, bowing his head and avoiding the Prince's eyes. It was clearly an icy start to the meeting. Once more the bare-headed black servant came over to the Shaykh and asked if he wanted coffee or tea. The Shaykh opted for tea with cardamom and sugar, which was promptly brought. Again this was a signal, as cardamom tea was usually served to relieve toothaches and miscellaneous oral pains.

"Now my brother, I suppose you would like to know the aim of this occasion. And I will tell you without chasing the mountain cat through canyon and hilltops. I want to ask you why you didn't come first to me to beg forgiveness before you made your unappreciated approach to our virtuous judges? Or why not appeal directly to the King's mercy? You have made a grave misstep, my friend."

"I beg Your Excellency's forgiveness. I acted rashly without thinking properly."

"That you did. Especially as your sinning offspring have not been charged or scheduled for trial yet."

"But of course, Your Excellency understands that when your beloved son and daughter face the bitterest of ends, you will go to the extreme lengths to save them from oblivion."

"And public shame." the Prince cut in. "But of course, it is not inevitable that your offspring must face the harshest public penalty. The judges still can apply discretion in their judgments—you know that well—and they have latitude. And there are still other things you can do for us that may be able to ameliorate your children's situation."

The Shaykh immediately recognized that he would have to perform something distasteful or odious for the Prince, perhaps even shame himself publicly in order to spare his children. He made no reply as he could not guess what the Prince would require of him.

"As you may know at this party last April, this debauchery staged by infidel foreigners who are guests in our county, that, in addition to your children shamelessly performing the most perfidious of sins as defined in the Holy Koran, there occurred also another abominable crime. Had you heard about the rape and murder of one of the young women who attended this party?"

"No, I had not heard anything about this myself. There have not been any reports in the press or gossiping about another such awful sin."

"That's right. There were no press reports of the murder allowed in the Kingdom. It occurred at the very end of the debauchery when most of the remaining guests were either sleeping or fornicating in rooms, so it went unseen by all, it seems." said the Prince as he scowled. "It is very distressing for me to even speak about such abominations." The Prince took out a linen handkerchief from one of his pockets and wiped his eyes as if he had been able to weep. But it was all a show. The Prince was trying to hide from his guests the appearance of gloating.

"Our very capable investigators, of whom Colonel Adil represents the very best, have been able to identify the culprit in this awful crime. And he absconded, fled from the Kingdom that very day, only hours after committing it. And he hasn't returned."

"Now this is the interesting part, dear cousin. It seems the killer, and rapist—a very evil, bad man in truth was—or should I say remains?— an employee of yours at your Bank. And I believe you know him well. And most interesting of all he fled on a very large yacht parked in the private marina in this city. A yacht owned by your Bank. And remind me Colonel Adil, what is this reprobate's name?"

"Captain Matthew Enders, a Scotsman." said Adil quick to come in at his prompt.

"Yes, precisely. That's it. Captain Matthew."

"Excuse me, Your Excellency, but I know no such a man."

"Please, don't dissemble and lie to me, dear cousin." said the Prince abruptly with iron in his voice. "We have monitored your cell phone calls in recent months and found that you indeed have called this Captain Matthew in Cyprus in early May. Several times. I think you cannot deny this."

"And interesting we found evidence that this man captained this boat and on earlier occasions he made voyages to Cyprus where he picked up cargos of illicit unmarked contraband and then brought them into this country, illegally, for your benefit. I think you know what I am talking about, so I will not go into detail just here. But we have plenty of evidence to show that you directed this illicit smuggling."

The Shaykh's face turned wan. He was looking at his feet.

"I would like to propose to you, dear cousin, a way to possibly save your beloved children from an end we all rightly abhor. Although they are seriously misguided and do need to be punished."

"I would like you to call this Captain Matthew and request that he return to the Kingdom with another consignment of your usual contraband on board. You can tell him that he should come back by the end of Ramadan, and that you need this contraband for the festive celebrations of the Eid at the end of Ramadan. Indeed, strongly encourage him to come by then. And ensure him that he will be safe. Because no one knows anything about what happened at the party. There have been no reports about it at all."

"I don't smuggle alcohol." said the Shaykh lamely.

"But see, you do, my dear cousin. I did not mention anything about alcohol." the Prince said as he smiled a twisted vindictive smile. "You just confessed."

"This way we can bring this horrible reprobate to justice, and make him accountable for the awful crimes he committed at that party. You do this for me, and Captain Matthew returns and then we might be able to relieve the awful and final sting of death from the punishment for your children's sins."

"Is that possible? Can the judges relent in passing capital punishment?" asked the Shaykh.

"Of course they can. Even more readily than they can through the encouragement of a large emolument. Isn't that so Sayyid?"

"Yes, the judges have wide discretion and latitude in sentencing on capital punishment." Sayyid Abdul Hamid answered. "And no one in fact wants to impose the most dreadful and extreme of capital punishments. There's a huge difference between a beheading and two hundred lashes, or even five hundred lashes."

"Do you consent? Will you call your employee and I might even say your friend, Captain Matthew, and request him to come back with a consignment?"

"I will try. But of course I cannot guarantee that he will come. He might never return to the Kingdom, if he thinks he will be tried and executed for murder."

"There are no guarantees in this life." said the Prince airily, waving his hand in the air. "We know that. God willing, you will convince him to return to Jeddah. We will listen to your telephone connections to Captain Matthew. You had better succeed."

The Shaykh looked at the Prince with malice in his eyes. He understood the threats. But he was threatened in any direction he took. His children faced the likely sentence of public execution by beheading or stoning if he did nothing. If he complied and Captain Matt agreed to come and brought the wine, he was certain that he would be arrested and tried for smuggling in illicit alcohol. They could take everything away from him, and leave him in prison indefinitely, for the rest of his life. He was certain that this was exactly what the Prince wanted: an irresistible trap that would bring him down. He could only see the possibility of fleeing the country. But then he could not save Adnan and Khadija, or his wife and his other children. He could only hope that Captain Matthew would not agree to come again, or even better that he would agree with the Shaykh on the telephone to come, but would then not come ever again to the Kingdom.

As he left the Prince's divan, Shaykh Abdullah cursed Adnan under his breath. But then he also began to curse Captain Matthew for being unable to control his vile, bestial appetites.

Adil left the divan also in a bad mood. He was shocked and disgusted that he had witnessed a set-up that would guarantee that justice would not be achieved all around as Sharia required. What he had just witnessed was the abuse of Sharia used for the Prince's political vendetta and personal enmity toward the Shaykh, and it was not becoming. It was not what he believed Sharia was all about, God's justice and mercy.

In Paphos

Captain Matthew sat under a sun umbrella idly daydreaming with a cold lager and staring out at the small waves lapping up on the beach just yards away from him across the road. It was late afternoon in late August and the sun was scorching hot. He had already drunk two pints of a strong English lager and was feeling the soporific effects of the alcohol, coupled with the heat. His mind drifted and his gaze remained fixed on the slate blue waters of the sea just beyond the white surf. Not even the shapely, bikinied young women walking or sunbathing on the thin strip of ochre colored sand attracted his attention.

The heat was stifling. And the sunlight blinding. He had spent now too many years in such a climate, and he no longer liked it at all. He wondered how he ever thought it was nicer living on the Costa del Sol, or in Cyprus or in the perpetual desert climate of Saudi Arabia than on the south Devon coast where he had grown up. He'd like to go back to Torquay, he thought. Maybe even if he had to go to prison. He could no longer tolerate the dry arid air and breathless days of summer in the dry latitudes around the Mediterranean. The skin on the back of his neck and on his arms was permanently a dark maroon color and wrinkled from all the time he had spent over his life in the sun. And when he thought about it, the bare land and coast lines of the Hijaz, or of southeastern Spain, or of Paphos where he was now idling, were not in the least attractive to him anymore. Even where the authorities planted palms and bougainvillea and kept them adequately watered. He just did not like the hot, sunny climates anymore, and he was close to admitting that he could no longer tolerate them. Maybe he could get a house in Switzerland and retire on the banks of one of those beautiful mountain lakes he had sailed on when he was in university.

But what would he do? That was the problem of his life in whatever direction he looked. He didn't have to worry about money for probably the rest of his years. He had no wife or family. He no longer had any employment obligations. And he no longer needed or wanted to live in Jeddah.

His wandering mind turned to visual memories of Anna on that last night together. In his mind's eye he began to recall her close in his arms as they danced together. She in white short shorts that enabled him to put his fingers up into her crotch and to stroke her clit. The aroma of salt and sweat on her neck as he kissed her there. And then later on the sofa out on the terrace, as he undressed her and she took his erect phallus out of his trousers. It was all like a dream at the time. He was re-living that dream just now. He caressing her tall, lean body, trying to remove her bra, and slowly moving over her as she moaned in pleasure. He saw how they moved up half standing against the low railing of the terrace and how she whispered to him, "fuck me, fuck me." And then the visions of Anna became fewer. His thrusting against her body, stretched mostly over the railing, and the coming climax. But then she was gone. His memory of the moment was of fumbling, of Anna's thrashing arms, a sudden jerk underneath him and his falling backwards and to one side back onto the terrace. No sound, no scream, no crash or thud on the ground below. He remembered scrambling back up and looking over the low railing. He could see Anna below, looking up at him helplessly, arms moving slowly and legs kicking and twitching. And then he remembered he was still ejaculating and mostly naked. He looked around him. There was someone there, a familiar looking undressed woman. But he couldn't remember who it was. The apartment was dark and empty, and no one apparently had seen them. He grabbed his clothes and then he fled.

He had had these memories often in the past few months. They haunted him day and night. Especially when he was too hot and a little drunk. But he didn't kill her. That much he always thought, as his memories played back in his mind's eye. He was sure of that. She had fallen. Lost her balance and fell over the railing backwards. She must have made a complete somersault to land the way she had. Poor girl, on those sharp metal prongs of the low fence.

He took another swig of beer. It was already beginning to taste stale and unpleasant to him; it was no longer fresh and icy cold. Anna had been special. He had not had a girl like her before in his time in Jeddah. It was too bad what happened to her. What an awful end for such a pretty, delightful girl.

And he thought again how he could not go back. He again thought he'd have to turn down Shaykh Adbullah's invitation and guarantee of safety. The Shaykh had called him on his mobile the other evening. He had told Matthew that the coast was clear and it was time for another delivery. He needed more stocks before the end of Ramadan, for the Eid holidays. Demand then was greatest. Couldn't he make it down to Jeddah by the end of the next week? Matthew had said he'd have to think about it. And the Shaykh said he'd call again today or tomorrow to get Matthew's answer. If Captain Matthew decided to go back he certainly wouldn't go to Addison's apartment again. He couldn't face that. No if he went again, it would be his last delivery to Jeddah. He'd sell his boat to the Shaykh, and he'd get on the first plane and leave Saudi forever, never to go back; he'd even abandon his apartment and all its furnishings.

A tall, dark haired and darkly suntanned woman wearing only a skimpy bikini which highlighted her breasts and her slightly pudgy tummy and the extra fat on her buttocks walked right across his gaze and interrupted his poorly focused day dreams and wandering thoughts. She was not even three meters from him. His eyes followed her as she ambled away on thin leather thong sandals. "Must be forty five, at least." he thought. "Trying to pretend to the world that she is twenty two and available." She had taken no notice of him. He was just another potbellied dirty old man sitting in the shade of the yellow umbrellas in one of the many bars that lined this narrow street on the waterfront of Paphos. There was nothing about Captain Matthew that would indicate to strangers passing by dressed in costumes meant to attract that he was a rich, unmarried dirty old man who was also a fugitive from the law in at least three countries. So she, like all the others that day and every day before that, paid him no mind.

He forgot about her as soon as the view of her swinging broad hips and jiggling round buttocks disappeared around an advertising tripod down the street. What was he thinking about? He needed to focus, but he couldn't. He needed to change this lukewarm beer for a better, colder one. Maybe if he changed brands it would taste better too. Having two or three of the same beer at the same time meant that there was no taste for the third beer, no matter how good the first one had tasted.

Then he recalled Anna's face the first time he saw her at the nurses' station in the King Fahd hospital. She had been in the standard light tan, loosely fitting uniform with long sleeves, and her hair was completely covered with a short tan turban that looked more like a shower cap than anything else. But her face just beamed. She had smiled at him in such a wonderful, happy way that his heart had melted. From that moment, not so many months ago, he had been smitten by her. He had to see her again, and again, as much as possible. She could not have been much older than his own daughter—whom he had not seen in fifteen years or more—but she looked so much prettier. And her expression was sincere. He could not have guessed from that first encounter that she was a blond, or even that she was Danish; her English was so good and unaccented. When Addison called him to invite him for that party and told him that Anna and some of her Danish friends from the hospital would also be coming, Matthew had not hesitated a moment in accepting. That's what he kept clearest in his memory. The first sight of Anna's face, beaming at him. No make-up on either eyes or lips, but just such unadorned beauty.

He ordered a half pint of a German brown ale, which the waiter assured him was very cold and on tap. He asked also as an afterthought for a starter of fried squid to go with it. The waiter asked if he could clear the half drunken pilsner and Matthew consented. But before the waiter brought these to the table, his mobile started squealing and bouncing on the white enamel table top. Caller ID showed that it was an unknown number in Saudi Arabia. Shaykh Abdullah no doubt calling back as he had promised. Matthew answered but there was no one on the other end, just a faint empty and hollow whining sound.

Again he thought about what he was going to do with the rest of his life. He was not old—he was only fifty-nine and still fit, strong, and in fairly good shape. But he knew he would not find work again, certainly not employment. Maybe he could run fishing charters. He knew how to do that. And he could even do that if he lived on a Swiss lake. He knew he had no future, regardless of where he ended up living. And the thought depressed him.

The waiter brought him his beer and small dish of fried squid, and set them gently on the table. And then he asked if he would like any ketchup or sauce. Matthew shook him away, just as his mobile rang again. This time it was the Shaykh.

"Captain Matthew, is that you?" said the soft voice in accented English. Matthew thought that when the Shaykh spoke English it always sounded to him like an Egyptian speaking English. It was a funny accent with far too many sibilants. Matthew wondered where Shaykh Abdallah was calling from. It was a strange time of day, nearly five o'clock in the afternoon; same time in Jeddah at that moment, and on a Ramadan afternoon. If Shaykh Abdullah was just then in Jeddah he would still be fasting or more likely napping.

"Where are you, Your Highness? Are you in the Kingdom this Ramadan? I forgot to ask the other day." said Matthew.

"Yes, I'm in the Kingdom. And I told you last time to drop the 'Your Highness' business. So have you thought about what we talked about last time? Will you come in about ten days' time?"

"I haven't really decided yet. You say you can guarantee my safety until I leave?"

"On God's book, I swear."

"I've decided that if I come, I'll sell my boat and leave the Kingdom for the last time."

"And walk away from all your friends?"

"Who would they be, besides yourself?" Matthew heard chuckling on the other end of the line.

"You've thought this out?"

"Yes."

"So will you bring the usual consignment?

"I can. But I haven't bought anything yet."

"So you'll agree to come?"

"I guess so."

"And you can be here before the end of the month? Before the end of Ramadan?"

"Yes." said Matthew. "But tell me: Why are you in the Kingdom this Ramadan? You usually go to the south of France. for as long as I've known you. You can't tell me your wife didn't want to go."

"Oh no. She went. With my brother and his family. But I've had work I had to get done here before the Eid holidays so I didn't go this year."

Matthew took this at face value. He was not thinking well, the beer had clouded his mind.

"Ok. So I'll come. I'll send you a message that I'm underway when I leave from Larnaca. Is that fine with you?"

"That would be wonderful. And it would please me to see you again after such a long absence. How long does it usually take you to sail down to here?"

"Most of four days. I stop off at Port Fouad and Port Suez. And if I need I might stop off at Yanbu'."

"No, don't stop in Yanbu' this time. The customs police might discover your cargo and then they would seize you and your boat. They're being especially watchful on Ramadan, this year."

They cut off the call. Matthew's stomach was feeling a little sour. He took another bite of a piece of squid, hoping its saltiness would help. He was also feeling too hot. He got up from his chair and the moist shirt on his back stuck to the seat back. He shouted to the waiter not to clear his dishes. He walked across the street and took off his shirt and shorts on the beach, revealing his swim trunks, and he stepped into the water to cool off. He walked out to where the water was up to his chest, but it was not a refreshing temperature. The sea water, blocked off from circulation from the deeper current by the breakwater two hundred meters further out, felt warm and sticky, even oily. And it smelled bad: like sea weed drying on the rocks, fetid and over-salted. As he was standing in the water, it reminded him of standing in the Red Sea waters with Daisy, his Philippine housekeeper in Jeddah several years before. More than a housekeeper she was his sexual partner and she kept him satisfied. He was reminded of her, and her very shapely brown body, because on a few occasions they had driven out miles from

Jeddah to a private, isolated beach, and they both used to stand naked together in the water up to his shoulders, about thirty meters out before the waves gained any height. And they would just stand in the water and pleasure each other. They never got caught. He loved those days, and could still see in his mind's eye her large breasts floating up on the salty water, as if they were brown balloons. If he tried the same thing even here in Paphos, there'd be a scandal. But those times in Jeddah, they were fifty kilometers from Jeddah, and they both risked death. For him the risk of being discovered had been really titillating and arousing, that threat of death that hung over them. Daisy probably did not really realize that she in publicly showing her sexual relations with him was in such peril. But he was so much younger then. And she was merely naïve. At that time, risk was something he valued.

Now on this late afternoon, he stood there in the warm water for twenty minutes, staring at the seedy bars that lined the beach road sixty meters away before he finally returned to the beach where he picked up his shorts and shirt and then walked to his seat at the bar. He needed to get into some air conditioning so he paid and started walking to his small flat on the hill behind the bar, taking the glass of beer with him. He was feeling old and hot, and fuzzy headed from the beers. He could not call up any further memories of either Daisy or Anna. His back ached, and he needed to piss. He thought about his upcoming trip back to Jeddah and then he suddenly thought also that he'd have to take his Glock pistol this time. But the thought slipped out of this mind even before he settled into the cooling chill of his room.

Ken's Ramadan Fast

After Ramadan began, conditions in Ken's jail cell became dramatically worse. He had suffered through most of the summer with the stifling heat and the suffocating humidity—there were neither air conditioning nor dehumidifiers working and there was only a small fan in his cell—but with the start of the Ramadan, he was appalled to learn that the Ramadan fast would be imposed on him. That meant that during the more than fourteen hours of daylight he was not given anything to eat. And worse and more dangerous for him he was not allowed to have any drink. He could only eat and drink at night, from the time when sunset occurred at around nine o'clock until the time of the dawn prayer at five in the morning. He was not told about this imposed fast in advance. The warden on his wing told him about it when he announced that there would be no food or drink brought that day because Ramadan had started, the new moon had been spotted the evening before.

Ken couldn't believe it: How could the Ramadan fast be imposed on a non-believer? And especially on one who was being kept against his will, in this infernal oven? He would die from loss of body fluids in just a few days. But there was no reasoning with the warden. "I do this on all my prisoners." he answered in his funny broken English. "I do as I told to do." Unlike like most practicing Muslims who observed the Ramadan fast, Ken had not prepared for this day with the large late night feast and copious amounts of sweetened drinks in advance of the day's fasting.

The first day was sheer misery. He spent the entire day prone in his cot, falling into and out of a troubled sleep. In the first hours he sweated as usual and his cot was soaking wet, but by the afternoon, he had stopped sweating and he realized that he could die from dehydration if he did not get some replenishment before nightfall. He was forced to keep still. He passed out completely several times in the afternoon. And to add to his misery, the wardens were slow to bring water when the signal sounded with the end of the fast for the day. He guzzled down the liter of tepid water he was given so fast that it upset his stomach. He ate the three small stewed dates as well and that helped settle his stomach. He then recognized the good sense of getting the "aperitif" of stewed dates as a way of breaking the fast, especially a long fast in summer. His dinner came about an hour and a half later. There was no communal dining hall in this municipal jail where he was being held, so he had had to take all his meals in his small cell, waiting on the wardens to bring his food and drink to him whenever they could. He recovered that evening a little from the heat exhaustion and dehydration he had suffered on that first day. But he declined the offer for some tea. He didn't need to drink any diuretics during the night, he realized. He had to conserve his body liquids to get through the day. He was awake and ready when at three o'clock in the morning before the dawn call to prayer the warden brought him a large meal which he thought strange included several desserts.

So he had survived the first day of the Ramadan fast. But the shock was still great on his body. Especially the dehydration which he suffered through every day during the height of the heat. To compound his suffering, after Ramadan started mosquitos started coming into his cell in the morning and evening twilight hours and began biting him mercilessly. After only a couple days, his the walls of his cells were smeared with blood splotches where he swatted those mosquitoes digesting their meals on his blood. He briefly worried about the possibility of getting malaria, as he had read that on the tihama coast around Jeddah there was endemic malaria. The daytime fasting also gave him by the end of the afternoon cracking headaches. On the second day he asked the warden if he could contact the local consul, Sir Philipp Angelsley. The warden said he would see what he could do.

Ken had read that it was normal in Saudi and Gulf Arab homes that the people who fasted gained weight during Ramadan. That this surprising result was due to the overeating of high caloric foods and sweets during the night when eating was allowed. But after a week, it was clear to Ken that he was losing weight. He estimated that he was not getting enough liquids and that dampened his appetite for the nighttime meals. He estimated he got only three liters of water at night and he was not allowed to ask for more, but he thought that he probably needed to take in more than twice that volume every day, especially as he declined the tea and he sweated so much. He repeatedly asked if he could get more water and tried to put some aside in the early morning before dawn, but each night all the utensils and bottles were removed from his cell. The Ramadan fast was being strenuously enforced on him, in a way that he was sure no Muslim faster had to submit to.

On his tenth day of Ramadan, Sir Philipp came to the jail and met with Ken. He brought with him two liter and a half bottles of water with him. "Are you surviving?" asked Sir Philipp. His question annoyed Ken. The interview room was air conditioned and was the most comfortable room he had been in for four months, but the consul wouldn't know that. "Barely. The water is much appreciated. I'm not getting enough." Sir Philipp was actually aghast at the sight of Ken, especially when compared to his appearance on the previous visit back at the beginning of May. Ken appeared wan and haggard, and his face had become more wrinkled and his eyes sunken. He also couldn't help noticing the red welts on his arms and neck, the clear sign of insect bites. But Sir Philipp courteously decided not to say anything about Ken's alarming appearance. Ken asked him when his case would be brought to court and what was the prosecutor's office thinking of charging him with.

"Quite right. Let me catch you up on what has been happening. It's not easy getting very clear information out of the prosecutor's office but I do have some news."

Then Sir Philipp related that Ken was probably going to trial after the Eid at the end of Ramadan. And although they, the prosecutor's office, had not decided precisely what charges they would present to the court, they seemed to be thinking of adultery and accessory to murder. That he potentially was facing capital punishment according to certain interpretations of sharia law.

"Murder?" asked Ken. "What is this all about? Accessory to murder?"

"It seems—you may have learned up to now—that your party ended in the murder of one of the Danish nurses who had been attending your party. She had also been raped, or had sex with one of the men attending the party—but not with you they assure me—who then flung her over the railing on your terrace. She was killed in the fall, in a most gruesome manner, I dare not tell you about. But the Deputy Head of the Investigations and Prosecution section, the man who came to your apartment—I should say, a very reasonable, enlightened man, American educated, not a religious fanatic at all—told me that they would continue to hold you without trial because you have persisted in not telling them who this man was at your party. You would probably not get sentenced to public beheading or stoning unto death if you told them his name."

"But I don't know." Ken interjected. "I didn't know the names of all the people who attended. I told them that. Some came as guests of other guests I had invited."

"This Inspector, Adil al-Kuthaimi, seems to feel that you are deliberating not revealing who the man was. That you are hiding him. If you were to tell me and I informed them in a way as if I got the name from my own inquiries well then I think they'll go easier on you and will wrap up your case rather more expeditiously."

Ken remained silent. The bastards. They were punishing him to get at Captain Matthew. He was sure that Matthew could not have thrown Anna over the side of the terrace. Perhaps he had sex with her. That was probably the case, but Ken didn't know that for certain. He hadn't seen them in any act of intimacy, he only saw Anna dancing with Captain Matthew. The only man's name he was deliberately withholding was that of Dr. Haidar. He didn't want to get him in trouble. As a devout Muslim, the authorities could really put the screws to him, just for attending his party, being in the presence of so much alcohol consumption and fornication. Then in a flash he thought that maybe they were harshly treating Bonny just as they were him to coerce a confession out of her. But he was very sure that Bonny did not know Captain Matthew's name, even if she had seen him, or seen him dancing or copulating with one of her girls. He had a momentary pang of guilt concerning Bonny's condition, caused by his reticence. Even though things had become bad between them in the past year or so, he did not want her to be harshly treated, or to have to suffer as he was.

"If we can tell Chief Inspector Adil, the name of that missing man, I think we can persuade them to give you royal pardon. Of course, you'll be expelled from the Kingdom. But a pardon, is a pardon. You'll be rid of this senseless suffering, and the threat of worse. And by the way, I can report to you that Bonny's already been expelled and is back in England. I haven't heard anything more about her."

Ken felt a momentary sense of relief. At least she is not suffering like he was. He would not wish this kind of torment on even his direst enemy.

"Maybe you'd like to write her a letter. I can convey it through our diplomatic channels and the Foreign Office would be sure she got it."

"I don't have pen or paper, nor an envelope here, so it would be difficult for me to write a letter." Ken finally said after a long silent pause as he looked at Sir Philipp with malice. He could see that Sir Philipp did not really understand the depth of Ken's suffering. And worse, it seemed to Ken that Sir Philipp was rather more sympathetic for the prosecutors.

"That won't be a problem. I will send over paper and come back to take the letter, before I go on leave in six days' time."

"And there is more news." Sir Philipp continued. "They sentenced the other three Danish nurses who were at your party to caning for adultery. They got twenty lashes in a private punishment, back in late June, before they were expelled. They also convicted a young American man. For adultery. He got thoroughly lashed by the cane. One hundred strokes, I think. I'm sure he's still smarting from that. They expelled him from the Kingdom, I believe, just before Ramadan started, not long ago. Too bad for the Saudi girl he slept with. It will go badly for her."

Ken knew who Sir Philipp was talking about. Khadija, Adnan's younger sister. Sir Philipp was right, if she were still living, the prosecutors would go after her with the sternest of punishments. But he was surprised to learn that Khadija had slept with Tony that night. He hadn't suspected before that they were a couple. She had always seemed to him to be so conservative and pious—unlike her brother—as well as shy and reluctant to talk to men. And he seemed to remember that Tony had left the party by himself to go home, late at night before Ken had taken Elsa to bed.

"I think I might write a letter. I'd appreciate it if you could get pen and paper to me. And if at the same time, do you think you might send me some mosquito repellent I could spray on. They are biting me every day without let up. And maybe some anti-infection cream as well. My scratching may have caused some infected welts."

"Won't be a problem. I'll do that by tomorrow."

"If the warden lets them get through and delivers them to me."

"Oh, I feel certain he will."

"What have you found out about my petition to get released on bail?"

"They prosecutors said they won't ask for bail for you. But they wouldn't tell me why. I suppose they are trying to pressure you for confessions and the other names at your party that you are withholding or don't know."

"Undoubtedly."

"I could use a lawyer, about now. Don't you think? I mean I thought the new laws stated that a man couldn't be detained for more than two months without being charged or brought to trial."

"I was told that a lawyer would be appointed for you when they have submitted the charges to the court."

"You're not telling me much that cheers me up. Not in the least. If Ramadan fasting doesn't kill me first, I think the mosquitoes will finish me off."

"We'll take care of you. Don't you worry."

"I suppose that means that you'll come visiting next time in another four months' time." Ken said acidly.

"Chin up, old man. Things will get better. Rest assured. We're talking at the highest levels of the Saudi justice administration, several senior princes, even, seeking your release. That's all we can be expected to do."

They got up to leave. Sir Philipp offered his hand and they shook. Ken paused and before he picked up the bottles of water and turned away, he whispered to Sir Philipp, "Captain Matthew Enders. He lived in a yacht in the marina." Sir Philipp nodded.

Ken went back to his cell clutching his two bottles of water. He intended to fight the warden for them if he tried to snatch them from him, but the warden took no heed of him or his two PET bottles. As soon as the door was locked behind him, Ken opened one of the bottles and took a long greedy draft of the water. He noticed that it had been chilled. It was a pleasure to violate the fast in the middle of the day. He would make it through to the evening "breakfast" without passing out.

Return voyage

In the port of Larnaca, Captain Matthew loaded up his hundred foot raised pilothouse motor yacht, the Chrysanthemum, with thirty cartons of French red wine and nine cartons of Johnny Walker Black whiskey. The yacht was his prize possession. He'd owned it for six years. It carried this cargo without a problem. In all he figured he had spent over $26,000 on the alcohol, less than his usual haul, but a volume that conformed with what Shaykh Abdallah had requested. The cartons were all unmarked; he bought them from a local Greek supplier on the condition that the cartons did not display any information about their contents. This particular supplier was accustomed to selling all kinds of alcoholic drinks to Muslim Arab countries and he had re-boxed everything in his inventory.

Matt also had hired a familiar face, a Greek from the Cypriot yacht set, to serve as his First Mate on the cruise down to Jeddah. He intended to sail day and night, and he needed someone he could trust to man the wheel while he got some sleep. Costa was such a man and he also knew the route. Matt bought him a return air ticket so that Costa would sail down one way and get a transit visa for Saudi. If their schedule went as planned, Costa would spend less than twenty hours in the Kingdom. Maritime crews usually did not have any problems with the Saudi authorities with getting such transit visas. Matt had a residence permit and a multi-entry visa in his passport—he traveled with a Dutch passport because his U.K. passport had long ago been revoked—so he didn't need to worry about entry or transiting.

Just as he had so often done in front of long voyages, Matt grew more and more excited and happy by the prospect of being on the open seas again. Admittedly the Red Sea coast was not very attractive—stark, basaltic and scorched bare rock were the terms that always came to mind when he thought about the coast. The coast of bones, he often thought. But he had never sailed the Red Sea for tourism. There would never be cruise ships going that way. Never mind the Somali pirates at the far end around the Gulf of Aden. It's simply that he adored sailing on the open sea with himself at the wheel.

He could have decided to sail back to Jeddah by himself just as he had when he had fled the Kingdom at the end of April because of the party. He had rushed to his yacht but with all the formalities of leaving port and passport control, he had not sailed from Jeddah until well after sunrise. And he was surprised at how difficult the boat had been to control at first. He had not realized until he cleared the last buoy that he was drunk. After he left Jeddah port, he had sailed first to Yanbu' and then to Port Suez. At both those ports he had berthed the yacht and re-fueled and gotten some sleep and refreshment. That voyage was a the most difficult he had ever made. He had started out drunk, and he was bothered especially by his escape from a crime. On the long stretches of open water he was frequently distracted by the memories of a pretty girl impaled on the fence.

He had made the round trip from Larnaca to Jeddah seven times before, a few times even when he had solo captained The Chrysanthemum. This time he would overnight at Port Said at the north terminus of the Suez Canal. It would take almost fourteen hours to sail there and then they had to wait eighteen hours or more because of the need to check in with the canal authority, pay his toll, get his place in line in the southbound convoy, and to re-fuel or rather to top up their tank. As a result, he berthed the Chrysanthemum in the marina and waited his turn. He and his first mate, Costa, had time to get a nice meal onshore in the town, and he even had a cold beer. Just as they went back to the boat, he radioed forward to the port master in Jeddah their anticipated arrival time and day. After dark their convoy left and cruised at a slow speed the one hundred and twenty miles down the canal. They emerged into the Gulf of Suez the next day in late morning, but instead of berthing in Port Tawfik in Suez Matt sailed on, planning to stop and overnight at Hurghada. As it was, they arrived near midnight at Hurghada where again they re-fueled and went ashore for the rest of the night. In the morning Matt checked the weather forecasts for the Red Sea. It was a favorable outlook, with north winds expected over the next two days. That would aid his crossing down to Jeddah. He figured it would take twenty five hours and since he wanted to pull into port in the early morning, figuring it was still Ramadan and that during Ramadan in the mornings things didn't work at all well in the port, then he should leave Hurghada very early in the morning on the next day. He would then get to Jeddah in the early morning as the city was sleeping. That was his ideal time for putting in. The night was only six hours long at this time of year and skies were clear and bright. So they did not have too long to sail in the dark.

But Ramadan equally dampened work efficiency in the Egyptian port and instead of leaving just before sunrise, they steamed off around nine in the morning. Matt was at the wheel for the initial six hours and to make up for the late departure, he set the speed at twenty-two knots instead of eighteen. The northerly winds held up as forecast. And as the coast sunk under the horizon Matt began to feel tired, a weariness that sleep did not help. He began to realize that he was becoming too old to drive a big boat like the Chrysanthemum by himself or with a minimum crew, especially voyaging on long stages. He had never felt this sort of weariness before. He even dozed off at the wheel a couple of times before his First Mate came to relieve him. Matt stepped out onto the rear deck and saw that there were dolphins riding along with the bow wave of his boat. It wasn't often that he saw dolphins in the open deep water away from the coast in this part of the central Red

Sea. The glare on the waters was intense and he couldn't stay long on the deck, so he went to his cabin.

And there he began to feel depressed. He had thoughts of increasing weakness and incapability. He thought again about his isolation and deepening old age. And he thought about the accidental death of Anna. He would never again meet another girl like that one. And he had killed her. These thoughts haunted him.

He tried to take a two hour nap, but only rested fitfully and had disturbing dreams. When it was his shift to take the wheel, twilight was slipping away and the sea looked like oxidized steel. At three in the morning as they approached Jeddah he would have to radio to the port master to advise him of his arrival. Over the following six hours everything was quiet and he turned on the radio to listen to open radio traffic. There were a few tankers that passed by them during the night. Their Philippino crews were chatting on the radio waves with other unseen ships. He began to think that he was sailing into a trap. That for some reason Shaykh Abdallah wanted him to return to Jeddah so that the police could arrest him. He couldn't understand why. Maybe the authorities wanted to shut down his alcohol imports, maybe they were still prosecuting Anna's death and wanted him for it. Finally, he radioed the port manager and asked him clearance to berth in about four hours. The port manager acknowledged Matt's request. "The passport control officer will come to your boat when you dock. You should go to your usual berth."

That was strange. Usually Matt would go to the border control office after he had berthed; sometimes even hours after he had tied up and turned off the engines. It looked as if they would not arrive at the ideal time of early morning on a Ramadan day, when no one wanted to work or would be at their posts.

He called his first mate to take the wheel and he left for his cabin to take a three hour nap after which he would come back and take the wheel as they made their final approach and to steer his big boat into the marina. As Matt came up from his cabin he took out the Saudi flag and he hoisted it from the foremast. Everything was in order. It was a bright, very hot morning and the winds had tapered off. The coastline was clearly visible as a dusty thick brown line on the horizon. After an hour the towers of downtown Jeddah began to appear through the brown dust.

Soon they would be in the harbor. The Chrysanthemum did not need a harbor pilot to pilot them in to their berth, but they could expect that their shipping agent would visit them as soon as they tied up. He would take all the documentation that Matt had to submit in order to put in to port and remain berthed. The passport and frontier control officers would come shortly afterwards. Then a representative of the port manager would come and inspect the boat to see that it was in compliance with Saudi port rules—the Saudi flag flying for instance and having the proper first aid and lifesaving equipment, proper gangways, and registered radio equipment.

But very soon after they were tied down and Matt had put on his Captain's jacket and put his passport in his jacket pocket and his handgun in his waist, Matt came up to the poop deck and began to look around. Everywhere in the leisure marina port it was still—as if everyone had fallen into a deep sleep. Costa joined him shortly after, also with his passport visible in his chest pocket. It was his First Mate's first visit to Jeddah, and indeed to any Muslim port in late Ramadan and he was spooked by the stillness in the port. But Matt was concerned that the usual routines were not happening. His shipping agent—a Lebanese man—had not yet shown up and should have come an hour earlier. And the passport control officers usually came out to the boat within an hour and a half and they were nowhere to be seen. Matt grew more and more agitated and worried. Something was wrong he felt.

Then after more than an hour waiting, Matt noticed a car pull up to the marina about one hundred meters away. Four men got out. They were in police uniforms and they moved leisurely, but in a manner that demonstrated that they did not know where they were going. But eventually they stopped by a port building and stood for a while there until they were joined by a man in a the more usual Saudi white dishdasha and keffiya. Then altogether they began making their way up the docks and piers toward the big boat dock and toward the Chrysanthemum.

This group of landlubbers eventually came up to the gangway stairs and the man in the dishdasha came aboard first. The others followed. They stood up on the middle deck about twenty feet from Matt and Costa and they looked at Matt. Adil stepped out from the group and raised his voice.

"You there, Captain Matt Enders, you are under arrest for the crimes…"

But Adil did not finish his statement. Matt drew out his Glock hand pistol and waved it in front of him. The three police officers behind Adil cringed and recoiled back, reaching for their service pistols. But then in an abrupt sweep of his arm, Matt drew the pistol up to his temple and pulled the trigger. He fell to the deck dead, a splatter of blood spray and brain pieces dripped slowly down on the railing next to him.

Three letters in after-thought

It was raining lightly that morning, the usual misty spray that seems to fall from the sky through all of the autumn days, and the emissary from the Embassy was late. They had told them that he would be driving from Copenhagen, not coming by train. Mikkel and his wife Karoline were waiting in their snug living room, well-lit in contrast to the gloom outside. They had put up a large photo portrait of Anna on the fireplace as a perpetual reminder of their loss. In it Anna showed a big smile, and looked genuinely happy. She would in the future be forever twenty-three years old in the memories of her parents because of this photo. They had used it, cropped and enameled, also on Anna's gravestone.

Life had changed so much for the Hansens since Mikkel had gone to Jeddah to collect the body of their only child. They both felt older and their future seemed to closing in on them. They felt more isolated than ever before even though they had not moved from their small house in Odense. They both still worked at the jobs they had had for many years, but now retirement seemed eminent. The savor of life had somehow slipped away and gone flat.

Mikkel went into the kitchen and made himself another tea and came back to sit with Karoline. He didn't mention it, he had stopped long ago raising the subject, but he was thinking again why it was that Karoline had never wanted another child. He could never understand her objections. Perhaps now she was even more devastated with the loss of her only dear girl. Mikkel noticed that in recent months Karoline would often sob in her sleep, or cry out Anna's name. She had never done that before. They had told the Embassy representative who had called that they couldn't meet with him in a restaurant or public place. Mikkel knew it was because Karoline would likely cry and she didn't want to be seen crying in public. She had appeared too often crying on the cameras when the news had first come out.

The doorbell rang. Mikkel stood and walked over to the door. He opened it and in front of him was a slight bare-headed man with swarthy skin and a small neatly trimmed triangular black beard. He was wearing a tan colored trench coat, so often seen in English spy movies. The front door did not face the street, but was on the side of the house in a narrow lane facing the brick wall of Hansen's neighbor's house, so Mikkel could not see the car the emissary had come in. The emissary smiled wanly and offered his hand to Mikkel.

"I'm Wa'il al-Masooudi, Consul of His Majesty's government in Denmark," the man said in perfect English. You are Mikkel Hansen I presume?"

"Yes, yes." Mikkel answered in slightly accented English. "Please come in, Mister Masooudi. "I'll take your coat here." Wa'il was dressed in a very elegant woolen suit.

In the living room Wa'il was offered to sit on the embroidered couch. He sat in the middle of the couch—his feet barely touching the wooden floor—and Mikkel thought he was the very picture of the little boy allowed to sit in the living room couch for the first time. But almost as soon as he sat al-Masooudi again sprung to his feet and went closer to Karoline.

"And this must be Karoline Hansen." He took her hand that she had offered to shake into his hands. "Madame I want to express my profound sorrow over the premature death of your beloved Anna. It must be an awful loss to you and your husband."

"Thank you." Karoline said softly. But she was thinking as she had often thought since hearing of Anna's death that Anna would probably still be with them if she had not been so supportive, so encouraging of Anna's wish to go to Saudi Arabia. Her husband had been strongly against the idea, and at the time when she left, his opposition had soured their relations. Now she could only blame herself.

"Can I bring you a cup of tea? Is it still Ramadan for you?" Karoline asked.

"That would be too kind." said Wa'il in his Oxbridge accented English.

Karoline was unsure if he meant by this expression that he was declining, or that he would very much appreciate it. She decided the latter and left the room to go to the kitchen. Wa'il again sat in the middle of the blood red couch.

While Karoline was out Wa'il asked Mikkel, "Did you bury Anna nearby? Do you visit her grave often?"

"Yes, we buried her in the churchyard of our local church. The Lutheran church. And we went only last Sunday after services."

Karoline returned promptly because Mikkel had no long before boiled the water in the kettle. She came bearing a small silver tray with a ceramic tea cup filled with black tea, a dish with two shortbread cookies, and a small sugar bowl.

"Oh thank you, so very much, Mrs. Hansen." And then pointing to the portrait, he continued: "I presume this must be a photograph of Anna? She was so beautiful."

"Yes, that was a photo taken about six years ago." said Karoline.

"I'm again so sorry. I come bearing this letter containing the official apologies of the Kingdom." And he abruptly reached into his suit jacket inner pocket and slipped out a long white envelope, offering it over to Karoline. The envelope seemed too full. It was official letterhead with the words the Ministry of Justice the Kingdom of Saudi Arabi printed in English in green ink in the upper left hand corner. Mr. Mikkel and Mrs. Karoline Hansen was typed in the middle of the envelope.

"Please open it." he prompted her.

Karoline took out two folded pieces of paper. The top sheet had printed in the upper corners the words, the Ministry of Justice of the Kingdom of Saudi Arabia, Riyadh in English in the left corner and in Arabic in the right corner. The letter was in written in English and it had an elaborate signature at the bottom as well as a seal with crossed swords in green ink. Karoline glanced at the second sheet and saw that it must be a Danish translation of the letter.

She read:

Dear Mr. and Mrs. Hansen,

On it is behalf of the government of the Kingdom of Saudi Araba, that I wish to express my profoundest regret and sorrow for the misfortunate and untimely death of your daughter, Anna Hansen, last April in Jiddah.

As is written in our laws and in our tradition, we will expend all our efforts to seek justice for your daughter's killing either through retribution and the severest penalty for the killer, or by offering to you the family of the victim compensatory wergild.

We have now determined Anna Hansen's killer, and we have after much effort apprehended him and condemned him.

It is because of this that we now are able to send you this wergild for your daughter's killing. Please find a check for one million Euros enclosed with this letter. We hope that this can compensate you both in a small way and help relieve some of the suffering that you doubtless suffer.

Again allow me to offer you the most sincere condolences.

In the name of Allah, All Justice comes from Allah, the most Gracious and most Merciful.

Yours truly,

Abdallah Ibrahim al-Shaykh
Minister of Justice

Karoline looked up and then handed the letter to Mikkel. She reached again in the envelope and pulled out a bank draft which indeed was made out to both of them in the sum of one million Euros. She passed the check to Mikkel who glanced at it briefly while continuing to read the letter to himself. Meanwhile she read the Danish translation. In both versions she got stuck on the word wergild. What an old-fashioned word and archaic concept. She wasn't sure what its boundaries or context were. Blood money just did not seem like a fitting way to compensate Anna's horrible death. And really could anyone compensate Anna's parents for their loss of their only child in such a terrible manner? No one could possibly compensate the pain that Anna had suffered, if even only in a few moments.

Mikkel also stumbled on the word. "Wergild? Is that specified in Saudi law?" he muttered to no one in particular.

"Yes. I understand. Would 'blood money' sound better? It is the idea that there must be retribution and retaliation for the killing of one's own blood and family. And besides death for a death, then the payment of compensation money for the loss of a family member—and obviously the economic value of a family member—is a long-tried method for retribution."

The room fell silent.

"But wergild? The very term sounds so savage, so uncivilized and barbaric, what the Vikings would have used." said Mikkel. "So much like in the Old Testament: an eye for an eye, a tooth for a tooth."

"Perhaps, but wouldn't you find it more civilized than decapitation? Especially, you here in Denmark who ban capital punishment out of moral distaste?"

"We don't believe in retaliation or vengeance in our punishments, at all." said Karoline. Nor in monetary compensation for damages. They can't bring Anna back to us."

"You would rather not accept this compensation, then? Of course, it will not restore Anna to you, but you could use it in support of what Anna most wanted to do. A charity, a foundation for nurses struck down prematurely with illness or paralysis, or a fund to pay for nursing for the indigent and homeless, or for scholarships for nursing or medical training for young women, or somethings like that."

Again the Hansens were left speechless. Wa'il up to that point hadn't touched the tea, and now he picked up the cup and took the tiniest sip. It was cold. He put it back down. And he began to look like he felt awkward and off balance.

After a long embarrassing pause, Karoline said: "Is this the address which we can use to send a thank you letter to the Minister?"

"Undoubtedly. You don't have to go through the Foreign Ministry. You can send such a letter directly to that address. It will be appreciated. And if you do write, it can be in English. It will be translated for him."

Finally, Mikkel broke the awkward silence. "Mr. Masooudi, I would like to thank you for coming all this way from Copenhagen to deliver this. And we thank you and the Minister for your expressions of condolences. We will think about what to do with the compensation money. In memory of our Anna. You know that she wrote us not long before the party that she really liked her work in Jeddah. She liked her life there. She thought she was doing something important and useful for the people there. And she also liked her social life there." Mikkel spoke slowly and carefully. "So maybe we can find some useful way to commemorate her with these funds."

Wa'il understood these words as the proper closing for his visit and he stood up.

"Well good, I will be leaving you now. As you say locally, 'Gud gor med dig I fred'—suitably accurately pronounced—which is close to our Ma'a salama."

Wa'il shook Karoline's hand and then went with Mikkel to the door where he got his coat. They shook hands and Mikkel opened the door for Wa'il.

"Thank you for your kind visit." said Mikkel. "Have a safe drive back."

He went back into the living room. Karoline looked at him and then picked up the check from the coffee table and slipped it into the frame of Anna's portrait. "Yes, we'll think of something."

As Wa'il slipped into the comfortable soft leather upholstery of the Embassy's Mercedes for the three hour drive back to Copenhagen, he saw that the skies were clearing a little and that now there were splotches of light blue in the sky. Blue skies and direct sunlight were what he missed most about home since he had been living in Denmark. He had lived in Copenhagen since just before the huge scandal when the Jutland Post ran the caricatures of the Prophet Muhammad in 2005. He was thinking that really, there were not many shared values between Denmark and his country. He'd never be able to understand or accept these people.

It was late October that year, a dreary, overcast typically rainy English day when the last of the leaves are blown off the trees in the Midlands.

That is when the house phone rang waking Bonny from her stupor. She had finished a fourteen hour shift at noon that day and desperately had been in need of sleep before going back to the hospital at ten that same evening for another ten hour shift. She hadn't even undressed or laid down in bed. She had sat down in the cozy, warm overstuffed chair in the main room and dozed off without any difficulty. She was getting too old to carry on the mind-numbing schedules of nursing.

"Yes, this is she speaking. Bonny Addison. Who is this please?"

"I see. Well you've found me now. What does the Foreign Office want with me? My misadventures in Saudi are over and thankfully forgotten."

"Do you have to visit? All the way out here?"

"Yes, I work in the Queen's Medical Center in Nottingham but I live out in Beeston, not in the city. I can appreciate that it was difficult finding me, but I would prefer any official visit to be at my house and not in the hospital. It's only a few miles away. Quite easy to find."

"No tomorrow would not work. During the day—let's see—well then not earlier than Friday. I'll be home and rested during the day. We can meet then. I would imagine that if you want to come up from London on the day we could not meet until after noon. So what is that drives you to come all the way up here to talk to me?"

"A letter? From Ken?" she asked and thought at the same time with a wry bit of sarcasm, 'that's rich of him to send a letter to me through the Foreign Office after he has nearly ruined both of our lives. She continued to think that any letter from Ken was bound to be filled with his typical whinging and recriminations. He was always blaming others, especially her, for all the woes he faced in daily life there in Saudi. "And you said a second thing. What else besides the personal letter?"

"Okay, fine then. You'll tell me what else on the day. Shall we aim for 12:30? I'll be expecting you then Mr. Manderley. It won't take long I suspect."

When Friday came there was a hard blow outside, although the clouds were still dark as they skittered by. She had stepped out in the morning and bought some shortbreads and small savories to serve with tea. When she came back she was chilled through and she noticed that her little house—a cottage really that she was renting from a distant friend—was also cold and felt damp. She turned up the feeble heater, but knew even as she did it that the house would not get any warmer by the time Mr. Manderley arrived. She sat in the warm overstuffed chair and pulled up a lap blanket over her legs and waited. Punctually, through the main window she noticed a swank black automobile stop on the street opposite her house. She could hear the crunching of shoes on the paving stones and then a sharp rap at the door. Three raps. She stood up and opened the door to a tall elegantly dressed man in a black Burberry coat. He completely filled the door—in fact he was taller than the upper lintel of the door and had to stoop to enter. Before she managed to close the door, she noticed that there was a driver in the car. He introduced himself and shook her hand and promptly offered her his visiting card. On it was printed John Sitwell Manderley. His family name was then followed by a number of clusters of letters that made no sense to her. But it was apparent that he was titled—and not merely academically.

"Yes, I see. Well, if you let me take your coat we can go into the sitting room where it is warmer and I have set out some tea and cookies."

"Splendid."

Then they were both awkwardly standing in the sitting room facing each other unable to make small talk, Manderley's head nearly touching the ceiling lights. She noticed he had huge hands. 'Must have been a rower at Oxbridge.' she thought sourly.

Finally she said, "May I pour you some tea?"

"Yes, that would be exceedingly kind of you on this raw day."

She poured out some hot orange colored tea in two china teacups that both had small chips on one side—it was her distant friend's china service—and put two shortbreads and one savory on the matching small dish and offered them to him.

He made to sip a bit of tea and then put the teacup down in its saucer. "Now to the purpose of this meeting." Manderley said gently as he reached into his dark blue jacket inner pocket. He drew out a letter that had one typed line saying Bonny Addison. "This is from your husband and was sent via our consul there in Jidder. (Bonny was surprised to hear what seemed almost a deliberate upper class mispronunciation of the city called locally Jiddah.) I have to apologize for the great delay it took to get to you. It was sent by diplomatic channels—and that caused some little delay—and then it took our London staff quite a while to find you."

"Yes, you said already. Over the phone."

"Well, still I must apologize for it being delivered with such a long delay. The mix-ups just continue to mount up in our office, I'm afraid."

Bonny handled the envelope as if it contained a poisonous white powder. "Shall I read it?"

"By all means. Do. But you don't have to read if out loud for my benefit. It's probably personal and best left private. Go ahead." Manderley picked up a shortbread and took a nibble.

Bonny easily opened the envelope, as if the glue on the back flap had been insufficient, or had been steamed open in transit. Then she took out the folded letter and shook it open to full length and began to peruse the document. It was handwritten and she recognized at once

Ken's crimped handwriting, very characteristic of a doctor she had always thought.

My dearest Bonny,

I write you from my temporary jail cell and it is Ramadan. It is ghastly hot inside and has been all summer too. From the beginning of Ramadan the jailers have imposed the fast on me, and I swear that on the first day I very nearly died from dehydration. I don't say this in whinging. It was true. I must have sweated two litres of water that first day and I didn't get anything to drink until seven twenty after sunset. I have since then stabilized, but I am still stewing in the infernal heat, and I have lost so much weight, I don't think I have been so light since when we were first married. But I don't mean to complain. Conditions here are horrendous. Mosquitoes eat me up but the consul promises to bring me some insect repellant and some balm, because I am scratching insect bites until they bleed.

I am still being held without definite charges, and I have not been visited by a lawyer yet. The consul tells me that the prosecutor's office refuses to allow me out on bail. They are probably holding me in this rat hole as punishment to coerce out of me the name of Captain Matthew. But I haven't told anyone. The consul also has told me the awful sentence that you got, but that thankfully you have been released and are presumably back in England. He says that his office is negotiating on my behalf for a reprieve, followed by expulsion. That I guess would be the best result. He hints that the charges that I am likely to face, when I finally get a hearing and a trial in front of a judge will be for adultery, for drinking alcohol and making alcohol—you remember we had a tub full of gut wrenching rioja stewing away when the police broke in?—for holding an orgy, and as an accessory to murder. This last charge I must say puzzles me. But I must say that the combined series of offenses are sure to mount up and result in the most dreadful of punishment. I dare write—as we have discussed many times before—I look to be bound to capital punishment and this will probably mean I will be beheaded. Publicly. At best I could get the caning of my life—unlike any I ever had in public school. You know that 500 lashes of the cane are not uncommon as we have seen first hand in KFC.

Like so many things about our life here in KSA the extremes I have outlined are both very possible outcomes, but like so much else, some combination in the middle of these two extremes is most likely. So maybe five more months in this hell hole followed by 200 lashes of the cane and deportation could be the likeliest outcome.

But in any event, I want to tell you because this may be the last opportunity that I have to do so that when we were first together I sincerely and deeply loved you. And that remained true even after I began seeing other women—mostly girls in the hospital that frankly I was seeking to shag for the sport of it. Even after our children grew up, I still maintained my love for you. But in the years before we left for Saudi I have to say I treated you very badly and that I am largely to blame for the increased disaffection that grew up during our eight years in KSA. I saw it that you had grown cold to me, but really it was my running around, chasing the skirts, that was to blame. I apologize with all my heart, and I know it hurt you tremendously, but in my self-centeredness then I just never cared at the time. I felt like I needed to hurt you and punish you. But I never imagined I could be such a monster to you. But I was. I was pushing you so that you would ask for a divorce and then I could be free with my life to get all the sex I wanted. But I never really thought I would by that be losing your love, forever. And what a disaster that would have been for me. Now I know all too well, and too later, that I cannot live without your love. And I dare say, I probably will not survive much longer without it.

So now I ask you, on my knees, even though in all likelihood we will never see each other again, to forgive me for being such a swine with you, for ignoring and insulting you, for believing that I had fallen out of love for you. Because I was so selfish. For all those times I deliberately tried to hurt you, feeling that you were ignoring and hurting me, please forgive me. I was wrong. And cruel and it all was so unforgivable. I cannot understand how you bore up with me for so many of the past few years. I say this knowing that our love will never be recovered, but I want you to know that I recognize more than ever before that it was once upon a time, and for a long time too, genuine and deep and sincere. And for that I deserve only your harshest reproach. Try to remember me as I once was when you by my side. It was I who abased our love and our marriage. And for that I want to tell you at what may be this last time, I am extremely sorry.

Please do not feel sorry for me. Now I must face my judgment and punishment.

I can only hope—and sincerely too—that you will find love again and that your life can be once more full of joy and fulfillment. And that the pain, torment, and grief I caused you for far too many years will eventually be washed away from your memory and truly forgotten.

Respectfully, (I would like to write your loving but you would know it would not ring as true), Your husband who caused you so much suffering, Ken

P.S. Could you tell our kids that at heart I was a good man, and that I loved them in my way?'

Bonny put the letter down in her lap. She was moved, her throat tightened, but it was difficult for her to cry. In front of this giant in her sitting room nibbling at shortbreads she just did not know how to feel. Ken was right in that her love and affection for him had evaporated in the Saudi desert years ago already. She appreciated that he was acknowledging his blame in so much that went wrong in their marriage. She had even been pushed to seek love in the arms of Walt, who turned out to be the wrong target. What a remarkable change in character for Ken to write all these things.

In an instant she had a vivid picture of memories from that last night, the party, that came back to her. The instant when Walt had left the party early without any apologies for his non-performance, for his lame display of affection. She had wanted to make love to him that night, she had wanted his kisses and for him to hug her and caress her, and instead he had just snubbed her affection as if she were some an old toad. And in her bitterness and rage, standing in the middle of the big room after Walt had left, she had turned around in the middle of the room—the divans and bedrooms all occupied by copulating couples, love-making. And she remembered then at once she had seen him humped that Danish girl out in the open, on the balcony in plain view. Really that was the last straw, to flout his shagging other women, that Danish slut—not her—so that all could see, oh the shame! She had rushed over out the terrace sliding glass doors which were wide open in a towering rage. All she could see was the twin cheeks of his bottom humping up and down rapidly on top of her, and she consumed by passion and moaning so the whole neighborhood could hear. And she remembered she was screaming at Ken, "How dare you disgrace me in front of the world!" And then she had grabbed him violently by his shoulders and jerked him away from that Danish slut and she pulled him back as if to face him and beat him in his face. But then when she did that, it was Matt! His curly red hair pasted to his forehead from sweat. A look of utter shock and dismay on his face. And in that same instant there was a little yelp and a slithering sound of moist flesh over stainless steel railing and Anna—not Elsa—in a flash disappeared over the rails and fell into the inky night. Bonny's memory of the night ended right there. She must have frozen in place. She remembered that Matt looked up at her with a look first of terror and then of alarm. She remembered that he jumped up quickly, peeked over the railing and turned back to her and said something like "What have you done?" then he gathered up his clothes, pulled on his undershorts and pants and ran out of the apartment. Every now and then in her dreams on nights when she was most exhausted Bonny again saw that instant when naked, steaming Mat looked up at her with that horrible expression on his face. On other nights, that even briefer rapid sequence appeared of Anna's arms flailing and her head falling back and disappearing below the railing in the flash of an eye.

All this came back to her in the briefest of memories after she completed reading the letter. She looked up again at Manderley who was sipping tea and looking at her expectantly.

"So. That is a letter indeed." Bonny said. "It's sad to read it at this distance in time and place. I suppose you've been briefed about the little party we had?"

"Yes, a bit of a bad spot, I should say."

"Yes, well you should say so. Very bad spot."

"Now, I am afraid that this second message —well everything was really mucked up by delays, incompetence, and crossed wires. Timing probably could be better. But we received again through diplomatic channels, a message from the Ministry of Justice of Saudi Arabia through their embassy here in London. They wrote a note. I will read it to you. It's very impersonal. And thank god its portent did not get into the press. They write:"

'The Ministry of Justice of the Kingdom of Saudi Arabia wishes to inform Her Royal Majesty's government in London that on October 2nd of the Western calendar year of 2008, or 2 Shawwal 1429, that a court in Jiddah heard charges against Dr. Ken Addison, a British citizen, for the crimes of adultery, accessory to murder, theft of medical materials, and conducting general debauchery, all serious crimes. He was found guilty of all these charges. He was condemned to death for these crimes and was punished by public beheading in front of the al-Maraqabah mosque in Jiddah on Friday, October 10nd of the year 2008.'

(Bonny's raised her hand to her lips to stifle a gasp of shock. Her face went ashen and her eyes grew wide. The letter in her lap fell to the carpet. Manderley continued.)

'We request that Her Royalty Majesty's government instruct us on whether it wishes to repatriate the body to the U.K. and to that end, give us instructions on how to proceed.'

Manderley put the paper with the note down on the center table next to the teapot.

"Let me say, Mrs. Addison, that I personally am very sorry for this horrible turn of events, and that I speak on behalf of all of my colleagues in the Foreign Office that we are all deeply upset and sorry, and commiserate with you for this sad affair."

"Why the rush from judgment to execution? Was there no appeal?" Bonny said as if talking to herself.

"We are looking into that question. And as soon as we received this note this past Monday, we put in the strongest of protests to the Government of the Kingdom of Saudi Arabia that this was unacceptable and that we should have been notified immediately upon the issuing of the verdict and sentence. I believe that our men in the Kingdom were working to get a royal pardon for Dr. Addison, and they had been led to believe that that was the likely outcome of this scandalous affair. But we were misled."

"This is really just too ghastly." Bonny said sadly and she now began to sob.

"I'd like to say that we did everything we could, but I know that we didn't and that we failed there in Saudi Arabia. We failed Dr. Addison and you, and all innocent victims of such barbaric punishments. And for that I also want to apologize on behalf of all my colleagues. We condemn such heinous capital punishment for almost any crime, and of course we condemn what seems to have been total lack of due process and application of justice."

"No, he was not guilty. Not either of adultery, at least as Muslims define it. There was no proof. And certainly not of accessory to murder. Whatever that means."

"We're looking into that too."

Manderley paused, but he did not move from the couch opposite Bonny, who continued to sob. Bonny reached for a paper handkerchief from a box that was next to the overstuffed chair. And she cried further into it, and then wiped her eyes once.

"I'd like to claim credit for our efforts of keeping this incident and its awful outcomes out of the press, but I think we can't claim credit there either. But I presume to say that you would want to keep this hush hush, and out of the public domain?"

"Yes, it will only lead to more uproar over things that we cannot anymore alter. Every journalist in the country will come after me. Because they can't interview the Saudis."

"The press In Denmark did report a little bit about the murder of that Danish nurse at the center of this story, but it did not go far and did not gather a big outcry." Manderley went on, even though Bonny was no longer listening to him. "We'll arrange to have the body repatriated."

Bonny looked out through the main window and in an unfocused way at the shiny black car standing in front of her house. The sun was now gleaming off its body. The blinding sun, like it so often was in Saudi, glinting off the shiny black metal. Then in her mind's eye she again saw Captain Matthew's face, his expression of terror and alarm, and his statement hissed at her, 'What have you done?' She had a momentary thought, 'What's become of Captain Matt?' But then she remembered the rage she had felt just moments before that instant on the balcony; rage aimed at Walt but above all a towering rage aimed at Ken.